FABLES

By

Shchedrin

[M. E. SALTYKOV]

Translated from the Russian
by Vera Volkhovsky

PELHAM LIBRARY

CHATTO & WINDUS

LONDON : 1941

SHCHEDRIN—SALTYKOV

1826–1889

When Nicholas I. sat on the throne of Russia, and a
soldier's military service lasted twenty-four years, when
serfs—termed souls for the transaction—were bought
and sold as live stock, when Bakoúnin was a boy of twelve,
and it was still two years before Tolstóy was born, the
greatest of Russian satirists made his appearance in the
society he was later to whip with a merciless tongue.

It was an age of extremes.

On the one hand ignorance, brutality, and oppression,
—a social order which worked as disorder built upon
exploitation and oppression as indisputable rights ; on
the other, an extraordinarily gifted educated class of
keen intelligence and lofty idealism ; and over this a
governmental system of crassly stupid dragooning, of
savage and ignorant repression.

The land-owning class, though supported in every
way by the government, was now irretrievably plunged
in debt. They were living in invertebrate indolence
on the labour of their serfs, who, without even sufficient
land to support their masters and themselves, were sent
frequently into forced labour in mines, factories, and
workshops. Corruption, incompetence, and a habit of
bullying was the rule among the officials, and there was
no redress against it, no appeal, for repressive autocracy
in its most rigorous form was the only government

Nicholas could understand, and death to all reform the only law he recognised. In the words of Geóukovsky, the Tsar saw the country not as a nation, but as a barrack.

Liberty was non-existent. The very word was forbidden in print. In 1849 the number of students in every University was limited to three hundred, the teaching of philosophy and metaphysics forbidden, while logic and psychology were declared to be the province of the theologians. Writers on mere suspicion of disaffection were forbidden to publish their works. None was allowed to leave Russia except by special permission of the Emperor, and a new Department of State was instituted for dealing with 'political' offenders, together with a special set of police, and an enormous system of espionage. Seventeen central censorship offices (and many lesser) worked with assiduity if not with understanding. Any suggestion of reform was instantly suppressed without even the appearance of justice and with the utmost savagery. The famous 'Petrashevtsy,' for instance (among them Dostoyévsky), were sent to hard labour in the mines and to Siberia although *no attempt at action* could be proved against them. Previously they were sentenced to death and made to undergo the preparations for execution ' to teach them a lesson.' The country was cowed into servile submission, yet in despite of this, opposition from below and from above broke out again and again. Risings of whole villages and districts were suppressed by armed force, there were five hundred such in

Nicholas' reign alone, and among the educated classes
there was formed the series of revolutionary organisa-
tions which from the Decembrists of 1825 onward
absorbed the progressive energies of the country.

After the demonstrated failure of the system during
the Crimean War, pressure of public opinion forced
Alexander II. to some attempt at reform—the most important being the liberation of the serfs—and Russia
breathed for the first time. The beginnings of political
life took firm root. But the radical period was short-
lived, and soon Alexander also returned to the traditional methods of government, though never in the same
degree as his predecessor.

Such was the Russia Saltykov knew. Poúshkin, Gógol,
Aksákov, Lérmontov, Koltsóv, Nekrássov, Chernishévsky,
Ostróvsky, Bielínsky, Hérzen, Bakoúnin, Tourgénev,
Dostoyévsky, and Tolstóy all lived within his lifetime.
Of these great writers only four did not experience
prison or exile. Chernishévsky spent twenty years in
the mines, while Tourgénev, Hérzen, and Bakoúnin
could exist only without the confines of Russia.

Born of the little nobility, an official by profession,
having held the post of vice-governor of Riazan and
then of Tver, by taste and education belonging to the
intelligentsia, Saltykov intimately knew all classes, and
after having at twenty-one been snatched into exile for
his innocuous first novel, developed into a powerful
writer of political and social satire. Under the pseu-
donym of Shchedrin he wrote a series of sketches, and
later some longer works ; he showed the unmitigated

tyranny above, the crawling servility below, the misty idealism of the reformers, the cowardice of the law-abiding. Yet he is no misanthrope. He is merciless but never unjust, bitter but never querulous ; his lash is directed with unerring aim, and invariably against the enemies of truth and of progress. Much of his work is too full of contemporary allusions to be of present interest, a great deal of it is wearisomely diffuse in style, partly from the necessity of concealing the truth from the censorship in a mass of verbiage—but the Fables form a kind of summary both of his ideas and of his art, and are, moreover, curiously modern and cosmopolitan.

In these Fables he castigates the society of his day, laying bare its weaknesses, its vices, its poor virtues, in a few touches of ridicule. Even himself he does not spare. ' Kramólnikov's Misadventure,' though of little artistic value, is of interest in giving us a figurative portrait of himself suffering under the ban of the censorship. ' The Carp ' might be a tragic parody of pre-revolution Russia, with the endless, well-intentioned theorist talk, while the whole explanation of the Revolution is in the story of the Two Generals. The beautiful ' Christ's Night ' is of directly political signifi-cance. In a country where, through the efforts of the ' Third Section ' (political police), the death, imprison-ment, or exile of the most intelligent and the most dis-interested was of daily occurrence, betrayal was a thing of immediate and terrible reality : was indeed the Unforgivable Sin. The tale of the newspaper-man is not out of date in any European country.

Stupidity and cowardice earn perhaps his most sting-
ing scorn, and these he shows us in every grade of
society, all subtly different, and all ludicrously true to
type. There is the stupidity of the official—in the
generals, one a touch stupider than the other ; of the
intelligentsia—in the carp : such a good fellow too ;
the cowardice of the bourgeois—in the rabbit, with his
weak nobility of motive ; the heavy, crass stupidity of
the land-owning gentry—in the squire ; of the parent
and citizen—in the fool's papa, who ' always looked as if
he were holding a pair of scales in one hand, and just going
to drop half an ounce of retribution in with the other.'

Shchedrin's spirit is characteristically Russian. The
ring of tragedy sounds through all his work, but of
poetry also, and of fun. Directness and sincerity,
bitterness, humour, savagery, and tenderness—that con-
geries of opposites bred in the Russian temperament by
an inheritance through centuries of suffering amid
nature and circumstances admitting of no compromise—
this we find in his Fables.

In ' Christ's Night ' and in ' The Fool,' for instance,
he shows that tenderness for the suffering of the humble
and the oppressed which is the very core of the
peasant's belief. In these two and in Ivànoushka of
' The Virtues and the Vices ' we have the popular
national conviction that the highest truth is most accessible not to the wise but to the childlike, with which
Dostoyévsky and Tolstóy have made Western Europe
familiar. ' The Poor Wolf ' and ' The Ram who could
not remember ' give that ring of tragic fatality and that

reach from the trivial to the profound which is a distinctive feature of Russian literature, the combination of realism and idealism which differentiates it from that of the West.

In spite of his directly didactic purpose Shchedrin is a real artist. His animal-humans—absurd, despicable, repellent, or pathetic—take visible shape: the generals, with their orders on over their nightshirts ; the rabbit, who so scrupulously had a bath before getting married ; the careful minnow, with his legacy of negative wisdom ; mamma, who whipped her fool so *very* gently ; the pathetic figures of the wolf and the ram, and the ghastly one of Judas. Not only do his men and beasts live, but in spite of the difference of place, time, and circumstance, his tales ring true to-day—indeed, will do while human nature lasts.

Shchedrin published his Fables at various times in contemporary Russian periodicals. Later they were collected and issued under the title of *Skaski* (Fables or Stories). There are altogether twenty-eight. In the following translation those have been omitted which have no interest to English readers.

Several of these translations have appeared in the *New Leader*, by the courtesy of whose Editor they are here reprinted.

VERA VOLKHOVSKY.

CONTENTS

CONTENTS

xi

FABLES

THE TALE OF HOW A PEASANT FED TWO GENERALS

Once upon a time there were two generals, and as they were both thoughtless, very soon ' by the pike's command, and by my wish,' as the saying goes, they found themselves on an uninhabited island.

The generals had held posts in some government registration office all their lives.[1] There they were born, brought up, and there they grew old, and therefore could understand nothing. They did not even know any words except, ' accept the assurance of my complete respect and devotion.'

The government office was closed down owing to uselessness, and the generals let out.

They took up their abode in Petersburg, in Podyachevskaya Street, in different houses : each had his cook and received his pension. But, suddenly, they found themselves on an uninhabited island. They woke up and saw that they were lying under one blanket. Of course, at first they did not understand it at all, and began to converse as if nothing had happened.

' A curious dream, your Excellency, I had last night,' said one general. ' I perceived that I was living on an uninhabited island.'

---

[1] They were what was called 'civil generals,' *i.e.* not officers but officials.—*Tr.*

He finished speaking, and suddenly jumped up. The other general jumped up too.

' My God ! what is this ? Where are we ? ' they cried with one voice.

And they began to feel each other all over to see whether it was not a dream, but whether really that such a mischance had happened to them. However much they tried to persuade themselves that it was nothing but a dream—they were perforce convinced of the saddening reality. Before them on one side stretched the sea—on the other lay a scrap of land beyond which they saw the same limitless sea. The two generals wept for the first time since the closing of the government office.

They examined each other carefully and saw that they were in their night-shirts, and hung round his neck each had an order.

' It would be nice to have some coffee now,' said one of the generals, but remembered what an unheard-of thing had happened to him, and wept again.

' What can we do, however ? ' he continued through his tears. ' If we write a report now—what use is it ? '

' Look here, your Excellency,' said the other general, ' you go east and I 'll go west, and in the evening we will meet at the same place ; perhaps we shall find something.'

They began to search for the east and the west. One remembered how his chief had once said, ' If you wish to find the east, stand so as to face the north, on your right you will find that which you seek.' They set to work to find the north. They turned this way and that.

They tried all the countries of the globe, but as they had spent all their lives in a government office, they found nothing.

' Look here, your Excellency, you go to the right and I 'll go to the left, that 'll be better,' said one general who, besides having been in the office, had also held the post of master of caligraphy in a school for soldiers' sons and was therefore rather brighter.

No sooner said than done. One general went to the right, and there he saw lots of trees growing, and on the trees all sorts of fruit. He did so wish he could get anyway one apple, but they all grew so high that it was impossible without climbing. He tried to climb up, but nothing came of it—he only tore his shirt. He came to a stream, and there the fish were just swarming—just swarming, as if it had been a pond in the Fontanka Garden.

' Ah, to have that fish in the Podyachevskaya,' thought the general, and his face grew positively sharp with the whetting of his appetite.

He went into the wood, and there grouse were calling, and woodcock, and hares running about.

' Good gracious, what a deal of food ! ' said the general, now even beginning to feel a little sick.

It couldn't be helped. He had to come back to the trysting-place with empty hands. And the other general was waiting there already.

' Well, your Excellency, did you manage to pick up anything ? '

' I found an old number of *Moscovskye Viedomosti*— that 's all.'

3

They lay down and tried to sleep again, but they couldn't go to sleep hungry. First they were troubled by the thought of who would draw their pensions for them, then they kept remembering the fruit they saw, the fish, the grouse, the woodcock.

' Who could have imagined, your Excellency, that human food in its original state flies and swims and grows upon trees ? ' said one general.

' Yes,' answered the other, ' I must confess I always thought that rolls were born in the condition you see them in at breakfast.'

' Therefore, if one wants to have turkey for dinner, one must first catch it, kill it, pluck it, roast it. . . . But how is it done ? '

' Yes, *how* is it done ? ' echoed the other.

They were silent and tried to go to sleep ; but hunger positively drove away sleep. Partridges, turkeys, sucking pigs, kept appearing before their eyes—juicy, slightly browned, with cucumber, pickles, and other garnishing.

' I think I could eat my own boot now,' said one general.

' Gloves are very good too, when well worn,' sighed the other.

Suddenly the generals looked at each other : their eyes burned with ominous fire, they gnashed their teeth, and from their throats issued a dull roaring. They began to creep slowly towards one another, and in another second they had flown at each other in rage. Bits flew, there was a sound of squeals and groans, the

4

general who had taught caligraphy bit off the other's medal, and instantly swallowed it. But the sight of blood flowing seemed to sober them. ' God save us ! ' both said together.

' But how did we get here ? What villain has played us this trick ? '

' We must distract ourselves with some conversation, your Excellency, or there will be murder here ! ' said one general.

' Begin,' said the other.

' Why, for instance, do you suppose does the sun rise first and then set, and not vice versa ? '

' How odd you are, your Excellency ! don't you rise first, go to the Department, write there, and *then* go to bed ? '

' But why can one not allow the following sequence : first I go to bed, see various dreams, and then rise ? '

' H'm . . . yes. . . . But I confess, when I worked at the Department, I always thought of it in this way : Now it 's morning, then it will be daytime, then they will bring dinner—then it 's time to go to bed ! '

But the reference to dinner plunged them both into dejection and terminated the conversation at the very beginning.

' I have heard from a doctor that man can live for a long time on his own juices,' one of the generals began again.

' How ? '

' In this way. One's own juices, apparently, produce other juices, these in their turn produce others again, and so on, until at last the juices stop altogether.'

5

And what then ? '

Then one has to take some kind of food.'

' Damn ! '

In fact, whatever the generals began to talk about, it inevitably returned to the mention of food, and this excited their appetites still more. They decided to cease conversation, and remembering the number of the *Moscovskye Viedomosti*, began to read it eagerly.

' " Yesterday," ' one of the generals read in a voice broken with emotion, ' " the respected chiefs of our ancient capital gave an official dinner. The table was spread for a hundred persons, with the most astounding luxuries. The gifts of all lands seem to have fixed as rendezvous this fairy feast. Here was served the ' Golden Sterlet from the River Sheksua ' and the nursling of the Caucasian Forest—the pheasant, and the fruit that is so rare in our Northern land in the month of February, the strawberry . . . " '

' Good God, your Excellency, can you not find another subject ? ' exclaimed the other general in despair, and taking the paper from his friend, read out the following :

' " We hear from Tulà : Yesterday on the occasion of the catching of a sturgeon in the River Oupà (an occurrence which has not taken place within the memory of the oldest inhabitants, especially as within the sturgeon was identified the Chief of Police) a fête was held in the local club. The hero of the occasion was carried in on an enormous wooden dish, surrounded by small cucumbers, and holding in its mouth a sprig of foliage. Doctor P., who was the chairman for the day, was careful to see that all the guests should have a piece. The sauces were various and even epicurean . . ." '

' Really, your Excellency, I don't think you are very careful either in your choice of subjects ! ' interrupted the first general, and taking the paper in his turn, read :

' " From Viatka they write : One of the oldest citizens has invented an original method of preparing fish soup : having taken a live turbot, first whip it, and when its liver becomes enlarged from chagrin . . ." '

The generals hung their heads. Every single thing their eyes rested on reminded them of food. Their own thoughts played traitor to them, for however hard they tried to chase away the picture of beef-steaks, the image forced its way into their minds.

Suddenly to the general who had been a master of caligraphy came an inspiration.

' What, your Excellency,' said he, ' what if we found a peasant ? '

' How do you mean—a peasant ? '

' Why, just simply—a peasant . . . an ordinary peasant. He would serve us up some rolls at once and catch us some woodcock and some fish ! '

' H'm ! . . . A peasant. . . . But how are we to get him, this peasant, when he isn't here ? '

' How " isn't here " ? There is always a peasant everywhere. One has only got to look for him. He must be hiding somewhere, shirking work ! '

This thought so heartened the generals that they jumped up instantly and began looking for the peasant.

Long they wandered about the island without the

least success, but at last the strong smell of chaffy bread and ill-cured sheepskin put them on the trail.

Towards the evening they came upon the hugest man, asleep, lying belly upwards, his fist propping his head, and evading work in the most shameless manner.

' Asleep, you lazy hound ! ' they fell upon him ; ' that 's all you care that there are two generals dying of hunger here these two days ! Off to work with you ! '

The man got up : he saw that they were severe generals. He tried to give them the slip, but they just froze on to him, grabbing him.

So he began to take action in their presence.

First of all he climbed a tree and picked the generals a dozen each of the ripest apples, and took one for himself—a sour one. Then he dug about in the earth and got some potatoes ; then he took two bits of wood, rubbed them together, and produced fire. Then from his own hair he constructed a snare, and caught a partridge. Finally he made a fire, and roasted so much food that it occurred to the generals that the lazy lout might be given some too.

The generals watched the peasant's efforts, and their hearts rejoiced. They had already forgotten that the day before they had nearly died of hunger, and thought to themselves, ' Ah, it 's a fine thing to be a general— you always come out all right.'

' Are you pleased, your Excellencies ? ' asked the lazy-bones meanwhile.

' Very nice, my man—we see you are doing your best.'

' Would you allow me to rest a bit now, your Excellencies ? '

' Do, my man, do, only make us a rope first.'

The man at once picked some wild hemp, soaked it in
water, beat it and crushed it, and by the evening the
rope was ready. With it the generals tied the man to
a tree so that he should not make off while they lay
down to have a sleep.

One day followed another : the man got so skilful
that he could even make soup in the palm of his hand.
Our generals grew merry, well-nourished, plump and
white.

They talked of how here they had free board and
lodging, and meanwhile in Petersburg their pensions
were mounting up and mounting up.

' Do you think, your Excellency,' one general would
say to the other after lunch, ' that the story of the Tower
of Babel is really true, or do you think it is just a
legend ? '

' I think it must be really true, or how else would you
explain the existence of different languages in the
world ? '

' Then the Flood must have really happened too ? '

' The Flood really happened, because how otherwise can you explain the existence of antediluvian
animals ? Moreover the *Moscovskye Viedomosti* informs
us . . .'

' Should we not read the *Moscovskye Viedomosti* a
little ? '

They would find the copy, sit down in the shade, and

9

read it from cover to cover, of how they ate in Moscow, in Tulà, in Pénsa, in Ryasàn—and would not feel sick a bit!

.   .   .   .

The long and the short of it was that the generals at last got bored. Oftener and oftener they began to think of their cooks left behind in Petersburg, and on the quiet they would even have a little cry now and again.

' I wonder what is happening in the Podyachevskaya now, your Excellency ? ' one general asked the other.

' Don't speak of it, your Excellency. My heart aches for it.'

' It 's very nice here, very, there 's no denying it, but still you know, it 's odd somehow, a ram without a ewe, and one misses the uniform too ! '

' Oh, doesn't one miss it ! Especially that fourth-class one. Why, just to look at the stitching alone, it 's enough to make you cry ! '

And they began to worry the peasant to take them to the Podyachevskaya. And lo and behold, it appeared that the peasant even knew the Podyachevskaya, that he had been there, had there drunk mead that ran down his moustache and never got to his mouth.[1]

' Why, we are generals from the Podyachevskaya,' they said, rejoicing, tremendously pleased.

' And I—I don't know if you 've seen a man hanging in a box outside a house, painting the wall, or walking about on the roof like a fly—that was me.'

And the peasant set to work thinking how he could

[1] A traditional folk-saying used in fairy tales.—*Tr.*

10

give pleasure to his generals in gratitude for the fact that they had been gracious to him, and had not despised his poor labour. And he constructed a ship—not exactly a ship it was, but a manner of vessel that you could cross the ocean in straight away to the Podyachevskaya.

' Don't you go drowning us though, you dog,' said the generals, seeing the boat rocking on the waves.

' Never fear, your Excellencies. It 's not the first time,' said the peasant, and began his preparations for departure.

He got some soft swansdown, and lined the bottom of the boat with it. Having finished, he put the generals in, and crossing himself, set out on his voyage. How many times the generals nearly died of fright from storms and winds of all sorts, how they cursed the man for his laziness—pen will not write nor tongue tell. And the peasant all the time went on rowing, and feeding the generals with herrings.

At last they saw Mother-Nevà and the splendid Ekaterinensky Canal, and now the Great Podyachevskaya !

The two cooks raised their hands to heaven when they saw how plump and white and merry their generals had become. The generals had some coffee, ate some sweet rolls, and put on their uniforms. They went to the Treasury, and the money they got out—pen will not describe nor tongue tell !

However, they did not forget the peasant either— they sent him out a glass of vodka and a silver penny. . . . There, go and have a good time, my man !

11

THE VERY WISE MINNOW

ONCE upon a time there was a minnow. Both his
father and his mother had been wise fishes ; they had
lived quietly for an age in the river, and never got into
fish broth, or down the pike's gullet. And they en-
joined their son, too : ' Mind now, my son,' said the old
father minnow as he lay dying : ' if you want to enjoy
life, just you keep your eyes skinned ! '

Now the young minnow had a deal of sense. He
began to cast about with this sound sense of his, and saw
that wherever he turned it was checkmate for him every
time. Around him in the water great fishes swam, and
he was the least of all ; any one could swallow him, but
he could not swallow any one. Nor could he understand
why he should swallow them. The crab could cut him
in half with his claw, the water flea could fasten on his
spine and torture him to death. And even his brother
minnows, directly they saw that he had caught a gnat,
would rush at him in a crowd to try and snatch it away.
They would seize it, and begin fighting with each other,
and just pull the gnat to bits for no good.

And man—what a cunning creature that was ! What
tricks had he not invented, to bring him, the minnow,
to an untimely death : nets, big and little, draw-nets,
and last, but not least—the fishing-line. You would
think what could be sillier than the fishing-line—a string,
and on the string a hook, and on the hook a worm or a
fly. And how are these put on too ? In the most un-

natural position you may say! And yet it is just with the line that the minnow most often gets caught!

His old father had warned him more than once about the fishing-line. 'Fear the fishing-line most of all,' he used to say, 'because, although it's the silliest sort of contrivance, yet with us minnows the silliest is the surest. They throw us a fly, just as if they wanted to be kind to us: you nip it up, and in that fly there is death!'

The old minnow also told him how once he had very nearly got into the fish broth. A whole company of fishers were catching fish there, they had cast nets across the breadth of the river, and went dragging them along a couple of versts on the bottom. What a crowd of fishes were caught that time! Pike, and perch, and dace, and pollard; even the lazy bream they lifted from the mud bottom! And as for the minnows—there was no counting them! And what terrors he, the old minnow, went through while he was being dragged up the river—pen cannot write, nor tongue tell. He felt that he was being taken along— but where he did not know. And there on one side of him was a pike, and on the other a perch; he thought every minute one or the other of them would eat him—but they never so much as touched him. . . . 'It was no time to think of eating, my boy!' Every one had the same in mind then: 'death has come!' but how and why it had come no one understood. At length the men began to draw the net in, dragged him on to the bank, and began to pour the fish out of the net

13

on to the grass. And here he learned what fish broth was. On the sand something red was quivering ; grey clouds streamed upward from it, and so hot it was that he went quite faint. He was feeling bad enough out of water—and here was still worse. He heard them call it ' fire.' And on the fire something black stood, and in it water seething and tossing, as in a lake during a storm. This they called ' a pot.' At last they said ' Throw some fish into the pot—that will make us some broth.' And then they set to, throwing in fish. A fisherman would pitch a fish in, it would go under, then jump out, as if it were half mad, then go under again and grow quiet. It had tasted broth seemingly. They went on and on throwing in fish—at first anyhow, then one old man looked at him and said, ' What 's the good of this little chap for broth ? let him grow a bit bigger in the river '—took him under the gills and tossed him into the water. And he being no fool made off as hard as he could swim for home. He got home, and there was his minnow wife peeping out from their hole, more dead than alive. . . .

And what do you think ? However much the old minnow explained and explained what fish broth was, and of what it consisted, there was seldom any one even now who had a proper notion of its nature.

But the son-minnow remembered his father's precepts perfectly, and took them well in. ' One must keep one's eyes skinned,' he said to himself, ' or one will perish ! ' and began to plan out his life. First he invented a special kind of hole for himself, so that he could

14

get out, but no one else could get in. He took a whole
year digging this hole with his nose, and what terrors he
went through during this time, spending the night in
the weed, or under a water-burdock leaf, or in the reeds !
At length, however, he made a fine thing of it—clean,
neat, and just room for himself alone. Then as regards
his life, he thought it out in this way : at night, when
men, beasts, and fishes sleep, he would take exercise,
and in the day he would sit in his hole and tremble.
But as one must eat and drink, and as he received no
salary and kept no servant, he would nip out at midday,
when all fishes were already fed, and by God's grace he
might pick up a gnat or two. And even if he had not
picked up anything he would go back to lie in his hole
and tremble. For it is better to have nothing to eat or
drink, than with a full belly to lose your life.

And this he did. At night he took exercise, bathed
in the moonlight, and in the day he got into his hole and
trembled. Only at midday he would dart out to get
hold of something—but what can you get at midday !
Every gnat at this time hides from the heat under a leaf,
every grub gets under the bark. He would just swallow
a little water and that was about all !

So he lay, day in, day out, in his hole, well-nigh
sleepless and foodless, and kept thinking, ' I *believe* I am
alive ! Oh dear, what will happen to-morrow ? '

He would doze off accidentally, and would dream
that he had a lottery ticket and had won two hundred
thousand. Wild with delight he would turn over on
the other side—and there, there 'd be nearly half his

head sticking out of the hole. . . . Whatever would have happened if there had been a young pikeling near by ? He would have dragged him out of the hole !

Once he woke up and saw a crab standing straight in front of his hole. The crab stood quite still, as if bewitched, staring at him with his bony eyes, only his whiskers moving with the current of the water. Didn't he get a fright then ! And half a day, until it was quite dark, that crab waited for him, and he meanwhile just trembled and trembled. Another time, he had just returned to his hole before dawn, just had time to yawn in pleasant anticipation of a snooze—when, from goodness knows where, exactly by his hole, lo and behold, came a pike gnashing its teeth. And it too watched him for a whole day, as if satisfying its hunger just by the sight of him. But he got the better of that pike too ; he just didn't come out of the hole, so there !

And this happened to him not once or twice only, but almost every day. And every day, trembling, he won victories, and every day he exclaimed : ' Thank God, I am alive ! '

But this is not all : he did not marry or have children, although his father had had a large family. He argued like this : ' My father could live like a duke ! In his time the pike used to be kinder, and perch used to leave us small fry alone. And although he did once nearly get into the fish broth, he happened upon an old man who got him out ! . . . But nowadays when a lot of the fish in the rivers are gone, minnows have become valuable, so it 's no use to think of a family—it 's as much as one can do to look after oneself ! '

And in this way the very wise minnow managed to live a hundred years. He kept trembling, kept trembling. He had no friends or relations : he went to see no one, nor any one him. He did not play cards, nor drink wine, nor smoke, nor run after pretty girls—he only kept trembling and thinking one thing : ' Thank God, I *believe* I am alive ! '

Even the pike in the end came to commend him : ' There now, if everybody in the river lived like this, how peaceful it would be ! ' Only they said that with a purpose : they thought he would come and pay his respects after that compliment—' here I am '—and then —snap ! But even that didn't take him in, and once more by his wisdom he escaped from the machinations of his enemies.

How many years went by after the hundred years no one knows, but at last the very wise minnow lay at death's door. He lay there in his hole and thought, ' Thank God, I am dying a natural death, as my mother and father did before me ! ' And he remembered the pike's words : ' If only everybody lived as this very wise minnow lives . . .' And what really would have happened then ?

He set to work thinking, for he had a deal of sense, and suddenly it was as if some one whispered to him, ' This way perhaps the whole minnow species would have disappeared long ago ! '

Because, for the continuance of the minnow species

first of all there must be a family—and he hadn't one.
But that wasn't all : for the well-being and strengthen-
ing of the minnow family, for its members to grow
healthy and robust, it was necessary for them to be
brought up in their native element, and not in a hole,
where he had grown almost blind from the perpetual
twilight. It was necessary, too, that minnows should
have adequate sustenance, should have social intercourse, should see something of each other and borrow
each other's virtues and other good qualities. For
it is only such a life can perfect the minnow species
and prevent it from deteriorating and becoming de-
generate.

It is a fallacy to think that only those minnows can be
accounted good citizens who, demented with fear, sit in
their holes and tremble. No, these are not citizens, but
just simply useless minnows. Nobody is any better nor
any worse for them, no one has the more honour, glory,
or dishonour . . . they live, truck up the place, eat up
the food. . . .

All this came to him so clearly and so vividly, that on a
sudden he had a passionate wish : ' I 'll just get out of
the hole and swim down the middle of the river like a
lord.' But scarcely had the thought occurred to him
than he was seized with fright again. And trembling, he
began to die. Living he trembled, dying he trembled.

His whole life passed before him in a flash. What
joys had he had ? Whom had he comforted ? Whom
had he given good counsel to ? Whom had he said a
kind word to ? Whom had he sheltered, or warmed,

or protected ? Who had heard of him ? Who remembered his existence ?

And to all these questions he had to answer, ' No one, no one.'

He had just lived and trembled, that was all. Even now he was at death's door and he was still trembling, he did not know why. His hole was dark, small, no room to turn in, no sunlight could enter it, no wave of warmth come in. And there he lay in this damp gloom, sightless, exhausted, wanted by no one—he lay and waited ; when at last would death through hunger finally release him from his useless existence ?

He heard how past his hole other fishes darted—perhaps minnows like himself, and not one took the least interest in him. Not to one did it occur to say, ' I 'll go and ask that very wise minnow how he has managed to live a hundred years, and no pike has swallowed him, no crab skinned him with his claw, no fisherman caught him with a line.' They went swimming by, perhaps not even knowing that in this hole the very wise minnow was concluding his life's history !

And what was most wounding of all : he had never even heard any one call him very wise. They just said, ' Have you heard of that dolt who scarcely eats or drinks, sees no one, has no guests, does nothing but carefully preserve his life ? '

And many even called him simply a fool and wondered how the water stood such idiots.

He lay thinking so and dozing. That is, he was not dozing exactly, but he had begun already to lose consciousness. He began to hear death murmur in his ears, and lassitude spread over his whole body. And he saw his former tempting dream, how he had gained two hundred thousand at the lottery, had grown to half a yard's length, and was now swallowing the pike himself.

And while he was dreaming this, his head, little by little, stuck out of the hole.

And suddenly he disappeared. What happened, whether a pike swallowed him, a crab struck him with a claw, or whether he died a natural death and his body rose to the surface, there were no witnesses to tell. Most probably he died a natural death, for what pike would want to swallow a sick, dying minnow—and such a *very wise* one at that !

THE CONSCIENCE IS LOST!

THE conscience got lost. As of old, people crowded into the streets and the theatres ; as of old, they got ahead of each other or were left behind ; as of old, they bustled about catching bits on the run, and no one guessed that there was something wanting, and that in the human orchestra some pipe had ceased to play. Many even felt freer and more vigorous. Man's ways became less difficult : it was easier now to trip people up, more comfortable to flatter, to cringe, to cheat, to tell tales, to slander. All 'malaise' suddenly vanished ; instead of walking, men seemed to fly ; nothing sad- dened them, nothing gave them cause to think—the present and the future alike seemed to be in their hands —the hands of those happy beings who had not noticed the loss of the conscience.

The conscience disappeared suddenly—almost in an instant. Only yesterday this troublesome, meddle- some creature had been whisking here and there before men's eyes, been appearing before men's imagi- nation, and suddenly—nothing ! The vexing appari- tions vanished, and with them went that moral disturbance which accusing conscience, the exposer, brought in its train. Now they had but to look at the good world and to rejoice ; the wise ones of the earth understood that at length they were free from the last trammels which hampered their movements, and naturally hastened to use the fruits of this freedom.

Men became bestial; robbery and violence reigned, and general ruin began.

And the poor conscience meanwhile lay on the road, torn, spat upon, trodden underfoot by the passers-by. Every one tossed it, like an old rag, as far from him as he could, and every one wondered how in such a well-appointed town a crying disgrace like this could be allowed to lie about. Who knows how long the poor exile would have so lain if a wretched drunkard had not picked it up, hoping in his tipsy condition that even this useless rag would get him a dram.

And suddenly he felt as if an electric current had shot through him. He looked about him with clouded eyes and began to feel quite clearly that his head was being freed from vicious fumes, and that the bitter appreciation of reality, upon the loss of which his greatest powers had been spent, was returning to him. At first he felt only fear—that dull fear which plunges a man into agitation simply from the premonition of coming disaster : then his memory hastily awoke, his imagination began to speak. His memory mercilessly dragged from the dark depths of his shameful past the details of the violence, the treachery, the feebleness of heart, the want of truth ; imagination created these memories into living forms. Then of itself awoke the power of judgment. . . .

To the wretched drunkard his whole past seemed one unbroken crime. He did not analyse, did not question, did not reflect, he was so overwhelmed by this picture of his moral downfall, that the process of self-judgment to which he voluntarily subjected himself punished him more heavily, more mercilessly, than could the most severe of human courts of law. He could not even take into account that most of that past for which he cursed himself so bitterly belonged not to him, the miserable drunkard, but to some secret monstrous force which blew and whirled him this way and that, as wind blows and whirls a tiny grass-leaf on the steppe. What was his past ? Why had he lived it thus, and not somehow else ? What was he himself ? To all these questions he could answer only by surprise, dismay, and the completest lack of comprehension. The yoke had fashioned his life, beneath the yoke he would go down to his grave. Perhaps now he was becoming conscious. But of what use was this to him ? Had it only arisen mercilessly to ask questions, and to answer them with silence ; only to make his wasted life once more flow into the ruined temple, now too weak to stand the force of its current ?

Alas, his awakened consciousness brought him no peace or hope, and his now active conscience showed him but one road, the road of useless self-accusation. He had been in complete darkness before, and now he was in darkness still, only now this was peopled with tormenting spectres ; his hands were chained before, and still those chains were there ; but heavier yet, for now he knew them to be chains.

The drunkard's fruitless tears streamed down his face ; the passers-by stopped and assured each other that it was wine which wept in him.

' Oh God. I can't—I can't bear it ! ' sobbing, cried

23

the wretched drunkard, and the crowd laughed and mocked at him. They did not understand that the drunkard had never been so free from vinous vapours as at that moment, that he had simply had a disastrous find, which was tearing his poor heart to pieces. If they had come upon this find themselves, they would of course have understood that there is an agony—most terrible of all agonies—that of suddenly acquiring a conscience. They would have understood that they too were as much beasts of burden, as maimed in spirit, as was the drunken man crying before them.

' No, I must get rid of it somehow, or I 'll perish like a dog ! ' thought the wretched drunkard, and was about to throw his find into the road, when the nearest passer-by stopped him.

' You 're employing yourself in surreptitiously distributing lampoons, I see,' he said, shaking his finger at him, ' you won't be long before you 're in jail for that ! '

The drunkard hastily clapped his find into his pocket, and went off. Peering about him, cautiously he approached the public-house, in which his old acquaintance Prohórich traded. First he peeped in at the window, then, seeing that there was no one in the public-house, and that Prohórich, quite alone, was dozing behind the counter, in the twinkling of an eye he opened the door, ran in, and before Prohórich could recover, the terrible find lay in his hand.

．　　　　　．　　　　　．　　　　　．

For some time Prohórich stood with his eyes starting

out of his head, then suddenly broke into a sweat. For some reason it seemed to him that he was trading without a licence, but looking about him attentively, he saw that his licence cards, blue, green, and yellow, were all there. He glanced at the rag in his hand, and it seemed to him familiar.

' Aha,' he remembered, ' why, this is the same rag that I had such hard work getting rid of before I bought my licence. Yes, that 's it ! '

Having come to this conclusion, he immediately for some reason understood that now he would inevitably be ruined.

' If a man is in serious business, and a rag like that gets into his hands, you may say he 's a goner—there 'll be no business and can't be ! ' he reasoned almost mechanically, and suddenly went white and began shaking all over as if a terror hitherto unknown had looked him in the eyes.

' What a mean thing to ruin the wretched people by drunkenness ! ' whispered the awakened conscience.

' Wife ! Arina Ivanovna ! ' he cried, beside himself with fear.

Arina Ivanovna ran in, but the moment she saw what Prohórich had acquired, she began calling out in a changed voice, ' Help, help, thieves ! '

' And why should I, through that scoundrel, lose everything in a moment ? ' thought Prohórich, referring to the drunkard who had given him his find. And great drops of sweat stood out on his forehead.

Meanwhile, the public-house was little by little filling

with customers ; but Prohórich, instead of pressing them
invitingly to drink, to their extreme astonishment not
only refused to serve them, but even tried most touch-
ingly to prove to them that in wine lay the root of all
misfortune for the poor.

' If you 'd drink just one little glass,' he said through
his tears, ' it would be all right—it would do you good
even ! But you try and guzzle a pailful at a time ! And
what happens at once ? You are dragged off to the lock-
up, there they will give you something under your shirt,
and you 'll come out as if you 'd had a reward, and all
your reward will have been a hundred lashes ! Then
just you think, my friend, is it worth your while to go
through all that and bring a fool like me your hard-
earned money ? '

' Have you gone off your head, Prohórich ? ' asked
the astonished customers.

' You 'd go off your head if this had happened to you,'
Prohórich answered. ' Just you look what sort of a
licence I 've got to-day ! '

Prohórich showed them all the conscience which had
been thrust into his hands, and invited those present to
make use of it. But the visitors, as soon as they knew
what it was, not only showed no disposition to consent,
but even shrank from him, and moved off a little further.

' There 's a licence for you ! ' Prohórich said with
spleen.

' What will you do now ? ' the customers asked him.

' Now, as I take it, there 's only one thing to do : and
that 's to die ! '

' That 's true enough,' they laughed.

' I think I had better break all these bottles and stuff here, and tip the wine into the gutter ! For any one that has this same virtue in him, even the smell of corn brandy will turn his stomach ! '

' You just dare ! ' Arina Ivanovna interposed at last. Her heart evidently had not been touched by the beatitude which had shed its light upon Prohórich ; ' there 's virtue for you ! '

But it was difficult to move Prohórich. He wept bitterly, talking and talking all the time.

' Because,' he said, ' if this same misfortune has happened to any one, he 's got to live in misery. And he doesn't have no opinion of himself as a shopkeeper or trader. Because that will be troubling himself for nothing, that will. But he has got to consider himself in this way : that he 's the miserablest man alive.'

In such exercises of philosophy the whole day passed, and although Arina Ivanovna resolutely opposed her husband's intention of breaking the bottles and pouring the wine into the gutter, still they did not sell a drop that day. Towards evening Prohórich even cheered up a little, and said to Arina Ivanovna, who was now in tears, ' Well, now, my soul, and my gracious wife, although we have made no money to-day, yet how light of heart is the man who has a conscience ! '

And indeed, directly he got into bed he went to sleep. Nor did he toss about, or even snore, as he used to do when he made money but had no conscience.

But Arina Ivanovna was of rather a different opinion

about all this. She understood very well that in a publican's trade a conscience was not a pleasant acquisition, and one which would not bring in money. She therefore resolved at all costs to get rid of the uninvited guest. She nerved herself to wait through the night, but as soon as daylight began to come faintly in at the dusty windows of the public-house, she stole the conscience from her sleeping husband, and ran out with it into the street.

As luck would have it, it was market-day ; from the neighbouring villages peasants were coming in with loaded carts, and the district police inspector Lovéts [1] was going in person to the market-place to maintain order. The moment Arina Ivanovna saw Lovéts, she conceived a happy idea. She ran after him as fast as she could, and directly she caught him up, with most amazing skill thrust the conscience into the pocket of his coat.

.   .   .   .

Lovéts was not what you might call an absolutely shameless fellow, but he did not like putting himself to any inconvenience, and used to plunge his hand pretty deep into people's pockets. He had not exactly an insolent air, but one of saying ' get off quick ! ' His hands were not too impudent, but readily grasped anything they found. In short, he was a pretty extortioner. And suddenly this man began to feel very uncomfortable. He came into the market-square, and it seemed

1 *Lovéts* means ' catcher.'—*Tr.*

to him that everything there—on the carts, on the stalls, and in the shops—was all somebody else's and not his. This had not happened to him before. He rubbed his shameless eyes and thought, ' Am I dazed, am I dreaming ? ' He went up to a cart, wanted to plunge in his great hand, and lo and behold, he could not lift his arm ; he went up to another, wanted to give a peasant a shaking by the beard, and oh horror, he could not stretch out his hands !

He was scared.

' Whatever has happened to me ? ' thought Lovéts. ' If I go on like this I shall spoil all my business ! Had I better not go home while I may ? '

However, he hoped it might perhaps pass off. He strolled about the market, and there all sorts of live stock was displayed, all kinds of material, and all of it seemed to say, ' Ah, near is the elbow, but you can't bite it ! '

And the peasants meanwhile grew bold. Seeing that the man was dazed, standing blinking at his own goods, they began to crack jokes, and to call him dolt, the son of a dolt.

' No, I must be ill,' thought Lovéts, and as he was, without a single bag, with empty hands, went home.

He went home, and his wife was waiting for him, thinking, ' How many bags will my dear husband bring me to-day ? ' And suddenly—not a single one. Her heart burned within her, and she fell upon Lovéts.

' What have you done with the bags ? ' she demanded.

' Before my conscience, I bear witness . . .' Lovéts began.

' Where are the bags, I am asking you ? '

Lovéts repeated, ' Before my conscience, I have nothing.'

' Well, then, dine off your conscience till next market-day. I have no dinner for you,' Mrs. Lovéts said with decision.

Lovéts hung his head, for he knew that Mrs. Lovéts was firm. He took off his coat, and suddenly seemed completely transformed ! As the conscience remained hung against the wall with the coat, he became once more light-hearted and care-free, and again it seemed to him that there was nothing in the world that was not his. And once more he felt the ability to wolf things up and to grab.

' Ah, now you 'll not get off, my friends ! ' said Lovéts, rubbing his hands, and began hastily to pull on his coat in order to speed to the market-place.

But—oh wonder ! He had scarcely put on the coat when again he began to feel uncomfortable. It was just as if he had become two men : one—without his coat— shameless, acquisitive, grabbing ; the other—in his coat —timid and shy. Yet, although he saw that he had lost his boldness even before he got outside the gate, he did not give up his intention of going to the market. ' Maybe I 'll get the better of it,' he thought.

But the nearer he got to the market, the more violently did his heart beat, the more insistently did he feel the need of making friends with all these people of small means, who struggled all day in the rain and the mud to get a few roubles. He no longer could trouble to look at other people's bags, his own purse in his pocket weighed him down, as if he had learned from reliable information that it contained not his but other people's money.

' Here are fifteen kopeks for you, friend ! ' he said as he came up to one peasant, giving him the coin.

' What 's that for, Mr. Dolt ? '

' For the harm I did you the other day, friend. Forgive me, for Christ's sake ! '

' God will forgive you ! '

In this way he made the round of the whole market-place and gave away all the money he had. However, having done that, although his heart was light, he felt he had food for serious thought.

' No, I must have caught some illness or other to-day,' he said again to himself : ' I 'll go home, and on the way take as many beggars as I can and feed them on what God sends.'

No sooner said than done ; he collected a crowd of beggars and brought them to his yard. Mrs. Lovéts raised her hands to heaven, and wondered whatever he would be up to next. And he went past her gently and said in a tone full of affection, ' There, Theodosia my dear, here are all these wanderers that you asked me to bring : feed them for Christ's sake ! '

But he had scarcely had time to hang his coat on the nail when again he felt light-hearted and care-free. He looked out of the window, and there he saw all the beggars of the town assembled in his yard. He saw them and could not understand why they were there. Was he to flog all that number?

'Who are these people?' he cried as he ran out into the yard in a rage.

'Who are they? They are all the wanderers that you told me to feed,' snapped Mrs. Lovéts.

'Send them packing, drive them off. Like this,' he shouted, and rushed like a madman into the house.

Long he wandered about the rooms and kept thinking what it was that had happened to him. He had always been an efficient man, as regards his official duties he had ever been a perfect lion, and now he had become nothing but a rag.

'Theodosia Petrovna, my dear, do for goodness sake tie me up! I feel to-day I shall go and do something that can't be undone in a whole year!' he entreated.

Mrs. Lovéts saw for herself that it was going pretty hard with her husband. She undressed him, put him to bed and gave him a hot drink. Only after a quarter of an hour did she go into the lobby, and thought to herself, 'I'll look in his coat, perhaps I'll find a copper or two still.' She turned out one pocket and found an empty purse; turned out the other and found a dirty greasy little bit of paper. She unfolded it, and her heart stood still within her!

'So that's what he's up to these days! Keeps a conscience in his pocket!'

And she began to think how she could get rid of the conscience—how she could hand it on to some one whom it would not weigh down altogether, but only cause him a little inconvenience. And she came to the conclusion that the best person for it would be the Jew, Samuil Davidovich Brgotsky, who used to be a government contractor and was now a financier and railway promoter.

' He 's got a thick neck, at any rate,' she decided, ' he may have a bad time for a while, but he 'll get through.'

So thinking, she carefully placed the conscience in a stamped envelope, addressed it to Brgotsky and posted it.

' Now, my dear, you may go to the market without fear,' she said to her husband on her return.

.   .   .   .

Samuil Davidovich sat at his dinner-table, surrounded by his family. Beside him sat his ten-year-old son, Rubin Samuilovich, performing banking operations in his head.

' Papa,' he asked, ' if I invetht that gold pieth that you gave me at twenty per thent, how much money thall I have at the end of the year ? '

' Thimple or compound interetht ? ' asked the father in his turn.

' Compound, of courth, papa.'

' If it 'th compound, and dithregarding the fracthions, it will make forty-five roublth theventy-five kopeth.'

' I 'll do it then, papa.'

' Do, dear child, only you mutht have good thecurity.'

On the other side sat Jossel Samuilovich, a boy of about seven, and he too was doing a sum in his head about a flock of geese flying overhead. Further on were

Solomon Samuilovich and David Samuilovich calculating what interest the latter owed to the former for toffy drops given on loan. At the other end of the table sat Samuil Davidovich's handsome wife, Lia Solomonovna, holding baby Rifochka in her arms, who was instinctively stretching out her little hands towards the bracelets which adorned her mother's arms.

In a word, Samuil Davidovich was a happy man. He was just about to partake of a wonderful sauce done up with something like ostrich feathers and Brussels lace, when the footman handed him a letter on a silver salver.

Scarcely had Samuil Davidovich taken the envelope in his hand, than he began to jump and fling himself about like an eel on live coals.

' But what ith thith for ? What do I want with thith ? ' he yelled, shaking in every limb.

Although no one present could understand the meaning of these cries, it became clear to them all that it was impossible to go on with dinner.

I will not here describe the torments which Samuil Davidovich suffered in the course of that memorable day : I shall only say that this little man, although physically delicate and weak-looking, heroically endured the most frightful torture, but would not return so much as a fifteen-kopek piece.

' What ith it ? It 'th nothing ! Only hold me tighter, Lia,' he begged his wife during his severest paroxysms ; ' and if I athk for the coffer, don't give it me on any account ! Let me die thooner ! '

But as there is no difficult situation in life from which

there is no escape, it was found even in this case. Samuil Davidovich remembered that he had long promised to give a donation to a benevolent institution under the patronage of a certain general of his acquaintance, but this had been put off day after day. And now, chance directly showed him the way to carry out his intention of long standing.

No sooner said than done. Samuil Davidovich carefully opened the envelope which had come by post, took out the paper from it with a pair of pincers, put it into another envelope, tucked in a hundred-rouble note with it, and went to his acquaintance the general.

' I with, your Exthellenthy, to make a donathion,' he said, laying the envelope on the table before the agreeably surprised general.

' Ah, that is very praiseworthy,' said the general. ' I always knew that you as a Jew . . . and according to the law of David . . . Dancing . . . singing . . . How does it go ? '

The general was muddled, as he did not rightly know whether it was David who made the laws, or some one else.

' Jutht tho, your Exthellenthy ! Only we are hardly Jewth,' returned Samuil Davidovich, now finally relieved ; ' we only *theem* to be Jewth, but our thonth are completely Ruththian.'

' Thank you,' said the general : ' I only regret one thing . . . as a Christian. . . . Could you not . . . eh ? '

' Your Exthellenthy, it only theemth tho. . . . Believe me, it only theemth . . .'

' Still ? '

' Your Exthellenthy ! '

' Well, well, go your way, and may Christ be with you ! '

Samuil Davidovich sped home as if on wings. By that evening he had completely forgotten the sufferings he had undergone and had thought out such an intricate operation to the undoing of all in general, that the next day every one's heart stood still when they heard of it.

. . . .

And for a long time the poor banished conscience wandered about the wide world, and many were the hands through which it passed. No one wanted to give it shelter, but every one, on the contrary, only thought of how to get rid of it, even if it were by fraud.

At last it was itself weary, poor thing, of having nowhere to lay its head, and having to live all its life among strangers and without shelter. So it prayed the man who had it last, a poor miserable little creature who sold dust at a street corner and never could get rich on it.

' Why do you persecute me ? ' complained the poor conscience, ' why do you harass and chase me from place to place ? '

' But what can I do with you, Lady Conscience, when no one wants you ? ' asked the wretched little man in his turn.

' I will tell you,' the conscience answered. ' Find me a little Russian child, open its heart before me, and bury me within it. Perhaps an innocent baby will shelter me and care for me. Perhaps he will keep me within him as he grows, and go out into the world and not be ashamed of me.'

And according to its word it was done. The man found a little Russian child, opened its clean heart, and buried the conscience within it.

The little child grows, the conscience grows with it. The little child will grow into a big man with a big conscience. And all injustice, treachery and violence will then disappear, because the conscience then will no longer be timid but will want to have everything as it wishes.

THE DECEITFUL NEWSPAPER-MAN
AND THE CREDULOUS READER

Once upon a time there lived a newspaper-man, and
there lived a reader. The newspaper-man was a deceitful creature—he took in people all the time; and the
reader was a credulous person—he believed everything.
It has always been so from the beginning of time—the
deceitful take people in, and the credulous believe it all.
Suum cuique.

The newspaper-man sat in his den, taking people in,
and taking them in, the whole blessed time. 'Take
care,' he would say, ' diphtheria is mowing the population down ! ' ' There has been no rain,' he would say,
' since early spring—as like as not we shall have no
bread presently ! ' ' Fire is destroying towns and
villages.' ' Government and private property is being
stolen right and left.' And the reader kept reading and
thinking that the newspaper-man was opening his eyes.
' Such freedom of the Press we have,' he would say;
' wherever you look it 's all diphtheria, or fires, or bad
harvests ! '

And so it went on. The newspaper-man soon jumped
to it that the reader dearly liked his deceits—and
straightway set to work gingering them up. ' We have
not the slightest security,' he said. ' Don't go out into
the street, reader,' he said : ' you 're sure to get into
the lock-up ! ' And the credulous reader strolled down
the road like a cock of the walk, saying to himself,

' Ah, how truly the newspaper-man has expressed this about our insecurity ! ' But not content with this : if he met another credulous reader, he said to him too, ' Did you see how beautifully our newspaper-man hit it off about our insecurity ? ' ' Why, of course I did,' the other credulous reader said, ' —inimitable ! One must not—one actually must not walk about the streets here —one will get put into the lock-up ! '

And everybody could not say enough in praise of the freedom of the Press. ' We did not know there was diphtheria everywhere,' the credulous readers cried with one voice, ' and just look at that ! ' And they got so light of heart from this confidence of theirs, that if the newspaper-man were to say there had been diphtheria but it was all gone, they would perhaps have left off reading his newspaper.

And the newspaper-man rejoiced—for deceit to him was clear gain. It is not every one who can get hold of the truth—just you try !—and you may have to shell out as much as ten kopeks a line for it ! But deceit now, that 's another story. Just write on and deceive away. Five kopeks a line—you 'll get stacks of deceits brought you from every side. And the newspaper-man and the reader struck up such a friendship, you couldn't have separated them with a pail of water. The newspaper-man, the more he deceived, the richer he grew (and what more does a deceiver want ?) ; and the reader, the more he was deceived, the more kopeks he brought the newspaper-man. However he sold his falsehoods, draught or in bottle, he went on making his pile !

' Hadn't a pair of trousers to his name,' the envious said of him, ' and look how he is going it now ! ' ' He has hired a flatterer now ! Has got a tame story-teller for himself, to tell him stories from peasant life ! He 's in clover ! '

The other newspaper-men tried to do him down with the truth. ' Perhaps the subscriber will rise to our bait too,' they thought. But not so. The reader would have none of it, but kept repeating :

> ' The falsehood that ennobles I hold dearer
> Than the innumerable base prosaic truths. . . .'

Well, so it went on, but at last there were found some kind souls who took pity on the credulous reader. They called in the newspaper-man and said to him, ' That 's enough, you shameless and untruthful man ! Up till now you have traded in falsehood, henceforth trade in truth ! '

And as a matter of fact, about this time the readers began to come to a little, and would send to the news-paper-man little missives like this : ' I went walking on the Nevsky with my daughter to-day, and thought to spend the night in the lock-up (my daughter even took some sandwiches with her on purpose—" Oh, what fun ! " she said). But instead we both returned safely home. . . . Now how do you reconcile this consoling fact with your leaders about our insecurity ? '

So, of course, the newspaper-man was only too glad from his own point of view. As a matter of fact, he had got pretty tired of deceiving them by that time. His heart had long been inclining towards the truth, only what can you do when the reader will rise to nothing but deceit ? You weep, you weep—yet you deceive ! Now, however, now that every one was at him to speak the truth, why, he was quite ready ! If it was to be truth, well and good, hang it all ! He had managed to acquire two solid houses through deceit, he would have to manage the other two solid houses through the truth !

And so he began to fill the reader up daily with the truth ! There was no diphtheria, so that was that. And there was no lock-up, and no fires : and if Konotop [1] had been burnt down, it was rebuilt better than before. And the harvest, thanks to the late warm rains, had turned out so splendid that we had all eaten and eaten to our fill, and then even begun to throw some under the table to the Germans :—may it choke you !

But what was the most remarkable of all—the news-paper-man printed nothing but the truth, yet still he paid only five kopeks a line. Truth had gone down in price since they had begun to trade in it on draught. Evidently, truth or deceit, it was all one—only worth a brass farthing. And the columns of the newspaper were in no wise the duller for this new departure, but even livelier. For if you begin properly to describe the mellifluous airs of idyllic peace you will get such a lovely picture that you 'd give all you possessed, and that would not be enough !

At last the reader finally came to and saw clearly. He was pretty well off before, when he used to take

[1] A town in the Tchernigov province. —*Tr.*

deceit for the truth, but now he felt completely easy in his mind. He would go into a baker's, and there they would say to him, ' I expect bread will be cheap presently ' ; into a poulterer's and they would say, ' I expect woodcock will cost nothing presently.'

' And what is it in the meantime ? '

' In the meantime it 's two roubles twenty kopeks the pair ! '

There now, what a change, with God's help !

And so one fine day the credulous reader strolled out, smartly dressed, into the street. He walked along in hope and glory, swinging his cane, as much as to say, ' Know that henceforth I am in complete security ! '

But this time, as luck would have it, the following took place : he had scarcely walked a few steps, when there occurred a judicial error—and he was put in the lock-up. There he spent the whole day without food. For, although they invited him to partake of food, he looked at it for some time and then just said, ' So that 's what our harvests are like, are they ? '

And there, too, he caught diphtheria.

Of course the next day the judicial error was cleared up and he was let out on bail (who knows, he might be wanted again). He went home and died.

But the deceiving newspaper-man is alive to this day. He is putting the roof on his fourth house, and from morning till night thinks of which is the handier way to take in the credulous reader—by deceit, or by the truth.

THE RABBIT WHO HAD THE HABIT
OF SOUND THINKING[1]

ALTHOUGH he was an ordinary sort of rabbit, yet he was very wise. And so well he used to reason—a match for the ass, any day. He would hide behind a bush somewhere so that he could not be seen and talk away to himself.

'Every beast,' he used to say, 'every beast has his ordained way of life: the wolf—his, the lion—his, the rabbit—his. Whether you are pleased with this life or not, nobody asks; you just live, and that's all. For instance, every creature eats us rabbits. You would think we would have grounds for objecting to that? But if you examine it reasonably, such objection is hardly valid. In the first place, he who eats us knows why and wherefore he eats; and secondly, even if we object with justice, we shall not be eaten any the less for that. More than is their need they will not consume in any case—but according to their need they will certainly eat. Tables of statistics issued by the Ministry of Internal Affairs . . .'

Here the rabbit generally went to sleep, as statistics invariably had the effect of rendering him unconscious. But he would have his sleep out, and then set to on a well-reasoned dissertation again.

[1] Shchedrin writes of the *hare*, which, far from having the aristocratic character conferred on him by the Squire's gun in England, is in Russia traditionally considered a low and mean little animal. I have therefore everywhere called him a rabbit.—*Tr.*

' They eat us, and eat us, and yet we rabbits just breed all the more, year in, year out. So just mind your eye with us rabbits! Summer or winter, look at the fields and you see rabbits scuttling all over them. We get into a cabbage patch or a field of oats, or near young apple-trees perhaps, and don't we give the peasant a time of it! Ah yes—you must keep a sharp eye on us rabbits, and no mistake. Why, the tables of Statistics issued by the Ministry of Internal Affairs . . .'

More sleep, more wakings, more sound thinking. . . . There was no end to the rabbit's wise havering, and he would add a little here, and guess a little there, and it all came out splendidly.

And what was so particularly valuable about it all, was that he neither had his eye on a career, nor was he trying to cut a dash before the Authorities by the originality of his views (he knew that the Authorities would, without listening to him, eat him), but he just simply loved— rabbit-like—seriously to reason things out. For—

> ' Ah, wrong are they who think that glass
> Superior is to minerals, Shouvalov. . . .'[1]

There, that 's how *we* do things!

He was sitting in a bush this way once, and had a mind to show off his sound thinking before his rabbit wife. Up he got on his hind legs and cocked his ears. With his front paws he set to work executing intricate figures, and off his tongue the words came rattling like so many peas.

[1] 'Epistle on the Uses of Glass,' by Lomonossov. — *Tr.*

' No,' he said, ' we rabbits could really live very well. We have weddings and dances and brew beer on holidays. We have sentinels round ten miles or so, and shout away. A wolf, hearing us, runs up : " Who was singing songs ? " Well, of course, all make themselves scarce. If you 've managed to get away, you can brew beer in another place ; if you 've not, the wolf will eat you as soon as look at you. And there 's nothing can be done about it. Wife, do I speak the truth or not ? '

' If you don't lie, you speak the truth,' the rabbit's wife answered. This was her tenth husband. All the other nine had died a violent death before her eyes.

' A wretched lot, these wolves,' continued the rabbit, ' —can think of nothing but robbery. Sirs ! Mr. Wolves ! Instead of killing a rabbit right off, you should just take the skin off him—in course of time he would tender you another. Though rabbits are prolific, still, if you take a heap to-day and a heap to-morrow, a rabbit in the market will have risen from twenty kopeks to half a rouble. Now if you were to take us properly in turn— " Mr. Rabbits, would you be good enough to furnish so many dozen for the wolf's dinner to-day ? " " Certainly, sir, certainly. Here, Elder—bring up those whose turn it is ! " And it would all go lawfully as it should. And both the wolves and the rabbits—they would all have satisfaction—on the one side and the other . . . oh, my dear sirs, my dear sirs ! '

The rabbit talked and talked till he began to wander —when suddenly he heard something rustling in the grass near-by. He looked. His rabbit wife had made off long ago, and there a tricksy fox was creeping on its belly towards him, for all the world as if it wanted to play with the bunny-rabbit.

' What a clever rabbit you are, now ! ' the fox opened the conversation. ' How nicely you talk—so sweetly, I could listen to you for ever ! '

He was a clever rabbit, but even he went numb for a moment. He stood there on his hind legs, rooted to the spot, looking out of the corner of his eye to see if he couldn't make off somewhere, and thinking, ' So this is how I 've got to take a reasonable view of my position. . . .'

' Hungry, Auntie ? ' he asked, trying not to be more frightened than he could help.

' Oh *dear* no. Not the least bit, my dear ! That may be later—but now not a bit. Good morning, Bunny dear. How are you ? '

The fox sat down dog-wise and invited the rabbit to sit down too, and he tucked his paws up under him. He tucked them up, and all the while kept saying to himself : ' Just exactly as I expected it has all happened. Every beast has its destiny : the lion his, and the fox hers, and the rabbit his. Now just get me out of this, my rabbit destiny ! '

And the fox sat there, seeming to read his innermost thoughts, and saying nice things to him

' And where has such a philosopher come to us from ?

' I came not so very long ago, Auntie, from three times nine leagues away. It was pretty comfortable in my little place there, I must say. Had a family, you know, and a little home and all that. In the winter we lived in the Squire's yard—lived royally. In the day we used to sleep, and at night we 'd have a go at the apples and the hops. It was getting on for Spring— time to be thinking of going off to the country—into the woods, when suddenly one day the wolf came. What are these animals ? By whose permission are they here ? I made off, to tell you the truth, but my mate with the little ones . . .'

' I heard about that. The wolf is a cousin of mine— and he was telling me. " The other day," he says, " I got a rabbit's home, the rabbit ran off. How do you think, cousin," he says, " we could catch him ? " And here you are the very one. You were sorry about your wife, I dare say ? '

' I don't remember now. I saw I had to be making off, so I just ran. I got here and met a rabbit widow. I said to her, " Let 's live together, you and I." So we did. Lived very happily, I must say. And now she 's made off and I am left.'

' Oh, you poor darling, you poor darling ! Well, give us time and we 'll catch her yet ! '

The fox yawned, gave the rabbit a light nip in the thigh (he, however, pretended not to notice it), rolled on to her side, tipped her head back, and shut her eyes.

' How that sun does scorch,' she murmured lazily, ' for all the world as if it were doing something useful. I think I 'll have a little nap, and you, meanwhile, sit up a bit closer and talk to me.'

So they did. The fox dropped off to sleep, and the

47

rabbit sat up close, so that at any moment she could reach him with her muzzle, and he began his tales.

' I am not particular, Auntie,' he said, ' I am willing to live in any kind of way. It 's scarcely three years I have lived in the world, and yet I 've run over the half of Russia already. You scarcely have time to get settled in one place—there 's a wolf, or an owl, or men after you at once. You 've got to run for your life, settle yourself afresh in some place three times nine leagues away. But I don't grumble at that, for I understand that such is the rabbit's life. And if sometimes I don't understand, then without understanding still I run. It 's like the peasants in our parts. Mikhéy may be just off to bed and there 's knock knock on his window. " Come on, Uncle Mikhéy—transport ! " A snowstorm outside, his miserable nag with scarcely a breath in it, but he loads up his sledge with soldiers, and off he goes twenty versts on foot beside it. In twenty-four hours he 's back again, with gingerbread for the children and a kerchief for his wife, and tears for every one in general. And ask him what 's the meaning of it all—he 'll tell you it 's the peasant's life. It 's just the same with us rabbits. We live—and don't do away with ourselves. We 're always in readiness. . . . Is it the truth I 'm telling you, Auntie ? '

The fox, instead of answering, gave a soft little bark, as if in her sleep ; the rabbit looked at her sideways—was Auntie really asleep perhaps? It may have occurred to him to make off if so. However, although the fox had not only shut her eyes, but had even rolled over on her back, the beggar, and spread her paws, yet the rabbit by instinct knew that she was just having him on.

' I will tell you,' he went on, ' how an uncle of mine once had a situation with a soldier. The soldier had caught him quite little, and taught him all the military ways. To fire a rifle, go through exercises, march, beat the réveillé—all this my uncle could do first-rate. They 'd go about together from fair to fair, and give performances, and the folks would make them a present of an egg here, a kopek there, for Christ's sake. This same soldier used to tell my uncle about his life. " I lived," he said, " at home with my parents, and once my father sent me to mend the sledge for the winter. I sat there mending it, singing to myself, smoking my pipe, and suddenly the village policeman comes into the yard. ' Go along to the volost office, Simèon—they want you for a soldier.' I went as I was—in the clothes I stood in —had the luck to have my pipe in my pocket. Went off, and twenty years I spent at it.[1]

' " And after that I came back to my place—not a stick or a stone left. . . ." That 's how it is,' added the rabbit wisely, ' with the peasant's life. One minute he 's a peasant, and the next a soldier, and each is called his life. . . . And so it is with us rabbits.'

' Do you mean they send you for soldiers too ? ' asked the fox as if she had just woken up.

[1] The rabbit is evidently speaking of very ancient times, when military service lasted at least twenty years, and recruits, lest they should escape on the road, were put into the stocks.—*Shchedrin.*

[This footnote of Shchedrin's is of course ironical, since the times to which he refers were only as distant as his childhood.— *Tr.*]

' No, they eat us,' the rabbit answered as gaily as he could.

' So I should think—because what sort of a soldier can you possibly make? Worse than the old guard which the famous general Bibikov used to call the " Good-for-nothing." And the soldier ate your uncle in the end, I suppose ? '

' No, the soldier died, and my uncle ran away then. He came home, but he 'd forgotten how to do proper rabbit's work, wasn't used to it. And my aunt was not willing to keep him without working. So he thought once, " I 'll go to the fair in the village and perform." But he had scarcely begun to drum out the cavalry trot when the dogs fell on him and tore him up.'

' Serve him right : shouldn't have troubled the public. However, your uncle must have known that sooner or later he was bound to be eaten—if not by the dogs then by the wolf or the fox. The end of you is all the same. But, tell me, what are the foxes in your parts like ? Fierce, are they ? '

' In our parts the foxes are, I must say, very fierce. I never met one at close quarters myself, but once saw a huntsman run one to earth in a field, and I must confess . . .'

The rabbit wanted to say ' I was very glad,' but pulled himself up in time and got a fright : however, the fox guessed what he was thinking.

' You bloodthirsty thing, you,' she said reproachfully, and bit his side so hard that the blood came.

'Oh!' squealed the rabbit with pain, but in a moment controlled himself and looked every inch a man. 'That only refers to the foxes in those parts, your exalted Highness—the foxes about here are kind, they say.'

'Is that so?'

'They are really. Last year we had a little orphan rabbit in our wood and a fox brought him up with her cubs, I've heard.'

'Brought him up, and let him go, do you mean? And where is he now then, your orphan rabbit?'

'Goodness knows where he is now. He has disappeared—got to thieving a bit, they say, into bad company, and at last betrayed a little vixen. And because of this the old fox, they say, ate him.'

'It was I ate him, I—I am the fox that you have heard about, but not because he got into bad company and led a vicious life, but simply because his hour had come.'

The fox fell into a reverie for a moment and rattled her teeth, catching a flea. Then without hurrying she got up, shook herself, and said in a perfectly good-humoured tone:

'And whom do you suppose I am going to eat now?'

He was a clever rabbit but he could not guess. Or rather, it flashed then through his mind, 'That's it—the rabbit's destiny . . . it's beginning!' but he was desperately loth to confess it even to himself.

'I don't know,' he answered. However, his face and

his voice so clearly betrayed him that the fox badly lost her temper.

'What a liar you are!' said she. 'They had told me goodness knows what about you—that you're a philosopher and a thought-reader—and here you are—the most miserable little bunny-rabbit. It's *you* I am going to eat, sir, *you*!'

The fox leapt back and made as if she was just going to spring upon the rabbit and eat him. But directly after, she sat down and unconcernedly began to scratch behind her ear.

'Perhaps now, you would let me off?' the rabbit said in a low voice.

'Whatever next?' the fox exclaimed, losing her temper still more. 'Have you ever heard of foxes letting rabbits off and rabbits getting let off? Do we live under the same sky just to play at letting folks off, you idiot?'

'Well, Auntie, there have been cases!' the rabbit insisted, keeping it up as well as he could. However, at this point his spirits fell and he lost heart.

He remembered how he had had to run from place to place, like a peasant of the Old Faith seeking the Heavenly City; how for days he'd had to go hungry, sitting shivering in an old hollow tree; how once, escaping from a wild beast, he jumped inside a peasant's coat—but luckily it was the time of the Great Fast, so the peasant let him go. He remembered his bunny loves with whom he brought up little rabbits, and how he had scarcely had time to breathe with any one of them. And remembering it all, he kept saying to himself softly over and over again :

' Oh, if only one could live a little—only just a little ! '

And the fox meantime had really prepared a nice surprise for the rabbit.

' Listen, you miserable rabbit-creature,' said she, ' I thought that you were really a philosopher, but I see the very thought of death crumples you up, so this is the chance I have thought of for you. I 'll go four paces off, turn my back, and won't look at you, miserable insect, for five whole minutes. And you meanwhile try and run past me so that I don't catch you. If you manage to slip off—you 've won. If you haven't, there 's the end of you.'

' Oh, Auntie, what 's the good ? '

' Stupid ! Even if you don't get off it 'll at any rate pass the time. You will have something to do. Just like a soldier at the front—he is getting his range all the time, and then all of a sudden it 's all up with him.'

The rabbit thought and thought, and was obliged to admit that the fox had hit on a good plan. To be gobbled up while in action is at any rate better than to be wearing one's heart out in uncertainty. The real rabbit death is just like that : you are running at full gallop, and suddenly—there 's an end of you !

' You don't understand what is happening to you, and all in a minute you are torn in two ! ' reflected the rabbit, ' and then perhaps after all . . .'

' Now none of these fancyings,' interrupted the fox warningly, guessing the faint hope that glinted through his mind. ' Just leave these fancyings alone. . . . One, two, three ! God bless you ! Begin ! '

Saying this, the fox took four steps forward, having first put the rabbit with his back to a patch of undergrowth, so that he could not possibly escape from the back, but would have to run right past her. And she meanwhile sat and occupied herself as if she were quite unaware of the rabbit. But he had no doubt that if she had gone even ten yards farther off, his minutest movement would not have escaped her. Several times he gathered himself into a ball, meaning to take a wonderful leap which would take him right away beyond persecution, but the conviction that the fox, looking at nothing, saw everything held him spell-bound. Nevertheless, the fox was right in a way : the rabbit had some kind of rabbitish occupation which did largely temper his agony.

At last the five minutes were up, and the rabbit sat motionless in the same place, wholly given over to the contemplation of this rabbitish business.

' Well now, Bunny, let's have a game,' the fox proposed.

They began.

For a quarter of an hour or so the fox jumped round and round the rabbit ; now she would bite him, and seem ready to tear his throat, and then she would leap aside as if thinking should she let him off ? But even that again was occupation of sorts for the rabbit, for even if he did not exactly defend himself, still, he covered his face with his paws, whimpered a little. . . .

But in a quarter of an hour it was all over. All that was left of the rabbit were bits of fur, and his wise words ' Every beast has his life : the lion—his, the fox—hers, the rabbit—his.'

THE OLD NAG

THE old Nag is lying by the roadside in uneasy slumber
The peasant has just unharnessed him from the plough
and let him out to have a feed. But the old Nag cannot
think of food now. It has been a difficult strip, full of
stone : he and the peasant have been hard put to it to
get it done.

The Nag is the usual peasant's beast : worn-out,
grievously beaten, narrow-chested. His ribs are sticking out, his shoulders sore, his knees broken. His head
hangs, his mane is matted on his neck, his eyes and nose
are running, his upper lip is flabby as a pancake. It 's
not much work you can do with a beast like that, but
work you must.

The livelong day the Nag does not get out of his
collar. In summer he tills the earth from morning
until night, and winter, before the thaw, he is carting
home-made wares. And yet there is no way for him to
get strength. His feed is only fit to clank your teeth on !
In the summer, when he is put out to night-pasture, he
can at any rate pick up some soft grass, but in the
winter he brings wares in to market and eats half-rotten
straw. In the spring, when they have driven the cattle
out into the field, he is lifted to his feet with poles ;
there is not a blade of grass in the field—only here and
there a little rotten old stuff that the cows' teeth missed
in the autumn.

It is a poor life, the Nag's. It is a good thing at any

rate that he happens to have a kind peasant for a master, who does not cripple him without need. They go out with the plough, the two of them : ' Well, old man, put your back into it ! ' the old Nag hears the well-known call and understands. He strains his whole miserable frame, pushes with his forelegs, shoves with his hind-legs, his nose on his chest. ' Go on, old wretch, pull it out ! ' And the peasant himself leans his chest on the plough, his hands grasping it like claws, his feet sinking in earth, watching the plough lest it cheats and misses a bit. They plough a furrow from end to end and both of them are all of a tremble : death, here it is ! Death for both—for the Nag and for the peasant ; every day—death.

The dusty peasant-road runs like a narrow ribbon from the village ; dives in among the houses, out again, and runs on heaven knows whither. And along its whole length, on either side, fields keep watch about it. There is no end to the fields ; they have filled the whole distance as far as eye can see : even where the sky has merged with the earth, there too is nothing but fields. Golden, greening over, or bare, they have gripped the village as in an iron vice, and there is no way out except into this gaping abyss of fields. There he is—man—walking in the distance ; his legs perhaps are giving way under him from hurrying so fast—and from afar it looks as if he were shuffling on the same spot, unable to rid himself of this overwhelming expanse of fields. It does not disappear into the distance, this small, scarcely discernible speck—it only fades a little. It fades and fades, and suddenly, unexpectedly, it is gone, as if the distance had sucked it into itself.

In age-long immobility lies the vast, motionless mass of fields, as if guarding magic powers within itself. Who will free these powers from their prison-house ? Who will call them out into the light ? This lot has fallen to two beings : the peasant and the Nag. And both from birth to grave struggle at this task. They run with blood and sweat, yet still the fields have not given up this magic force—the force that should unbind the peasant's bonds and heal the Nag's sore shoulders.

The Nag is lying full in the sun. There is not a tree near—the air is so hot that it makes you catch your breath. Now and again puffs of dust will rise from the village-road, but the wind which raises them brings not freshness but a very deluge of heat, again and yet again. Horse-flies and gnats rush madly to and fro under the Nag's belly, fill his ears and nostrils, bite into his sores, but his ears just give a twitch now and again at the stings. Is the Nag dreaming, or is he dying?—one cannot guess. He is not able even to complain that his very vitals are scorched up by the intense heat, destroyed by intolerable strain. Even this comfort God has denied the dumb beast.

The Nag is dozing, and over the agony of suffering which he has for rest, waft not dreams but a disjointed overpowering nightmare—a nightmare devoid of forms, even monstrous forms, but only masses, now black, now fiery, which stay or move with the exhausted Nag, and draw him after them farther and farther into a bottomless pit.

There is no end to the field—you cannot get away from it anywhere ! The Nag has walked it up and back with the plough, and still it has no end. Bare, or flowering, or motionless under its white pall, it stretches imperiously its length and breadth ; it does not call one out to battle against it, it simply enslaves one. There is no guessing its riddle, nor subduing it, nor exhausting it : now it is dead—now it is born anew. There is no understanding which is death and which is life in it. But of its death and of its life the first witness is the Nag. For all others the field means freedom, poetry, space : for the Nag it means slavery. The field oppresses him, takes his last strength and still never has had enough. The Nag trudges on from sunrise to sunrise, and before him goes a wavering black mass, and draws him on. Now too it moves waveringly before him, and even now through his uneasy doze he hears a voice call out : ' Get on, my hearty, get on, you devil ! '

It will never go out, that ball of fire which from morning to evening pours down torrents of blazing rays upon the Nag : never will cease rains, storms, winds, frosts. Nature is mother to all—to him alone she is a scourge, a torturer. Every manifestation of her life is martyrdom for him, every flowering—poison. There is no harmony of sounds for him, no lovely scents, no beauty of colour : he knows no sensations save those of pain, of weariness, of misery. The sun may fill all earth with warmth and joy, its rays may call others to life and happiness, the

Nag knows only that it adds but one more pain to those innumerable pains of which his life consists.

There is no end to the work ! Work is the sum total and meaning of his existence. For this he is conceived, for this he is born, and but for this he is wanted by none, indeed his thrifty master knows he is a loss. His conditions are all directed solely to one end : to prevent the exhaustion of that muscular force in him which gives him ability to work. Of food and rest he is given only so much as makes him able to struggle through his task. After that, the fields and the elements may maim him— no one cares how many new sores he has on his legs, his shoulders, and his back. The important thing is not his well-being, it is a life which will stand the burden of hard work. How many ages has he borne this burden he does not know, how many ages he has yet to bear it he does not reckon. He lives as though sinking into a black abyss, and of all sensations which a live creature is capable of feeling, knows only the gnawing pain of intolerable overwork.

The Nag's whole life is branded with the mark of endlessness. He does not live, yet also does not die. The field, like some great monster with many tentacles, has fastened on him and will not let him go from his destined strip. Whatever chance may bring him, he remains ever the same ; beaten, exhausted, half-alive. Like this field which he waters with his blood, he does not count days, nor years, nor ages, he knows only eternity. He is the same in every field, here, there, and everywhere, stretching to the utmost his miserable frame, always and ever the same, the nameless Nag. An indeterminate mass lives within him, undying, indivisible, indestructible. There is no end to life—that much only is clear to the mass. But what is this same life? Why has it bound the Nag in the chains of eternity? Whence comes it, whither does it go? Perhaps some day the future will bring an answer to these questions. . . . But perhaps it too will remain as dumb and unconcerned as that dark abyss of the past which has filled the world with ghosts and sacrificed the living to them.

The Nag is dozing, and past him Dandy-prancers [1] stroll. No one at first glance could tell that the Nag and the Dandy-prancer were sons of one father. However, the tradition of this relationship has not yet wholly died.

In times gone by, there was an old horse, who had two sons: the Nag and the Dandy-prancer. The Dandy-prancer was full of politeness and sensibility, but the Nag was crude and insensible. For a long time the old horse put up with this crudity, for a long time he brought up the sons in the same conditions, as a loving father should, but at last he lost his temper and said, ' This is my will towards you for ever and for ever: the Nag shall have straw—the Dandy-prancer oats.' So it was from that time forth. The Dandy-prancer was put in a warm stable with soft straw on the floor. He had honey-mead to drink and corn in the manger. The Nag was brought into a stall with half-rotten straw to eat: ' Champ your teeth, old Nag! As for drink— out of that puddle, there.'

[1] The Russian means literally ' Empty dancers.'—*Tr.*

The Dandy-prancer had quite forgotten that he had a brother, when on a sudden he got a fit of depression and remembered him. ' I am tired of my warm stable,' he said, ' I am sick of the honey-mead, I can't do with any more corn, I will go and see how my brother is getting on.'

He went to see, and lo and behold, his brother was immortal ! They beat him with anything they could lay hands on, and still he was alive ; they fed him with straw, and he was still alive ! And whatever part of the field you looked—everywhere his brother was at it ; he was here just now—and in the winking of an eye he was at the opposite end, working those old legs of his. There must be some kind of virtue in him, that you can break a stick over him, yet never break him.

And so the Dandy-prancers began walking round the Nag.

One says : ' You know the reason that nothing does for him is that from constant work there is a great store of commonsense in him. He has understood that ears don't grow above the forehead, that you can't break an axe-head with a rope, and lives quietly, quietly, all wrapped about with proverbs as cosy as may be. Good luck to you, old Nag ! Do your work ! Be watchful ! '

Another objects : ' Oh, indeed, it is not commonsense that has given his life this strength and permanence. What is commonsense, after all ? Commonsense is something ordinary, clear and definite to the point of revoltingness. It is like a mathematical formula, or a police order. It is not this which gives the Nag his indestructibility, but the fact that he bears within him the spirit of life, and the life of the spirit ! And while he contains these two treasures, no stick can destroy him ! '

A third observes : ' What awful nonsense you people talk ! " The spirit of life, and the life of the spirit "— what is that but the idle transposition of meaningless words ? That is not the reason for the old Nag's invincibility. It is that he has found his " real work." This gives him mental equilibrium, it makes him at peace with his conscience, both with his own and with that of the masses, and it endows him with that tenacity, which even years of slavery have not been able to overcome ! Labour, old Nag ! Stand firm ! Push on the ground ! and draw from work that clarity of soul which we Dandy-prancers have lost for ever ! '

And a fourth (who had evidently gone from the stable straight to the public-house) adds : ' Oh, gentlemen, gentlemen, you are completely out. It is not in the least anything special within him that makes the old Nag resist being done in, but simply because he is accustomed from time immemorial to his vale of tears. You can break a tree against him now and he will still live. Here he lies—and looks as if there was not a breath of life in him, but tickle him up properly with a whip, and he 'll go making figures with his legs yet. Whoever is appointed to a piece of work, does that work. Just count how many of these cripples there are a-wander among the fields here, all exactly like one another. Cripple them as you can, you will never make them fewer. One moment he is gone—the next he has come up again out of the ground.'

And as all these conversations were engendered not for any object, but simply from depression, the Dandy-prancers would talk a little and then begin to quarrel. But luckily just then the peasant would always awake and put an end to all discussion by crying : ' Hi, you ! you jail-bird, get on ! '

Here all the Dandy-prancers would catch their breath with delight.

' Look, look ! ' they would all call out with one voice, ' look how he stretches his poor old body, how he pushes with his front legs, how he digs his hind hoofs into the earth. That 's something like ! Stick to it, old Nag. That 's the creature to teach us ! This is he who is worthy of emulation ! Go-o on, then, you jail-bird, go-o on ! '

THE CARP WHO WAS AN IDEALIST

THE carp was arguing with the gremille. The carp was saying that one could live in the world by Truth alone, but the gremille declared that one could not get on without a bit of artfulness. What exactly he had in mind by the expression 'artfulness' is not known, but each time he used the word, the carp exclaimed indignantly :

'But that's dishonourable !'

To which the gremille replied :

'Well, you just see !'

The carp is a quiet fish, and prone to idealism : no wonder the monks are fond of him. He lies mostly at the very bottom of a river creek or pond, where it's quietest under the mud, and gets out minute shellfish from it for his provender. Well, naturally, lying there quietly, hour after hour, he thinks out something now and again. Sometimes something very free and bold even. But as carp do not send their thoughts up to the censor, nor register them at the police station, no one suspects them of being politically unreliable. And if sometimes we do see that now and then men catch carp, it is not for their freethinking, but because they are good to eat.

They are caught mostly with casting-nets or draw-nets ; but to have a good catch you must have knack. Experienced fishers choose the time immediately after rain, when the water is muddy, and then, casting the net, they strike the water with sticks and ropes, and generally make a noise. Hearing the noise, and thinking that it heralds the triumph of free ideas, the carp rises from the bottom and begins to enquire if he too cannot somehow join in the triumph. And that 's just how carp in great numbers get into the net, afterwards to fall a prey to man's gluttony. For, I repeat, carp make such a delicious dish (especially when fried in sour cream) that leaders of the nobility are ready to offer it even to Governors.

As regards the gremille, that is a fish already tainted with scepticism, and moreover prickly. Cooked in fish soup, it gives an inimitable bouillon.

How it happened that the carp and the gremille met, I do not know ; I only know that having once met, they immediately began to argue. They argued once, and then twice, and then got quite a taste for it : would make appointments with each other. They would meet somewhere under a water-burdock leaf and begin to talk wise talk, and the white-bellied dace would play round near them and pick up wisdom.

The carp always began it.

' I don't believe,' he would say, ' that strife and quarrelling is the normal law, under whose influence all that lives on the earth is to develop. I believe in peaceful, bloodless success, I believe in harmony, and I am deeply confident that happiness is not the vain imagining of fantasy, but that sooner or later it will be within the reach of all.'

' You can wait till you get it then,' the gremille would say sarcastically.

The gremille spoke with abruptness, restlessly. It is a nervy fish, evidently remembering many an injury. Its heart is so full—so full! It has not got as far as hatred, yet faith and naïveté are long gone. Instead of a peaceful life he sees strife everywhere, instead of progress, a general savagery. And he declares that he who intends to live must take all this into account. The carp he considers being ' a bit balmy,' but at the same time realises that he is the only creature one can ease one's heart with.

' And I *will* wait, and I 'll get it ! ' the carp would reply. ' And not I alone—every one will. The darkness in which we swim is the product of a tragic historic fortuity ; but as nowadays, owing to recent investigations, this fortuity can be exhaustively analysed ; the causes which gave birth to it can no longer be considered irremovable. Darkness is the accomplished fact, light the discernible future. And there will be light. There will ! '

' Then, according to you, there will come a time when there will be no more pikes ? '

' What pikes ? ' the carp would ask wonderingly, for he was so naïve that when he heard people say, ' There are pikes in the sea so that carp should not dream,' he used to think that they were mythical things like mermaids to frighten children with, and of course wasn't a bit afraid.

' Oh, you ninny, you ! You want to solve world-problems, and have no notion what a pike is ! '

The gremille used to wave his fins contemptuously

and swim off home ; but after a little while the companions would again meet in some retired spot (it isn't very amusing in the water), and again begin a discussion.

' In life, Good plays the most important part,' pronounced the carp. ' Evil is allowed just . . . just by a misunderstanding, but the principal life-force is still contained in Good.'

' Yes ! Open your mouth and shut your eyes.'

' Oh, gremille, what absurd expressions you use ! Open your mouth and shut . . . Now, *is* that an answer ? '

' To tell the truth, you don't deserve to be answered at all. . . . Stupid—that 's what you are, and there 's all your answer ! '

' But do just listen to what I am going to tell you. That Evil has never been a creative force, History itself gives us ample evidence. Evil stifled, suppressed, gave over to fire and sword, but the creative force was always Good. It hastened to the aid of the oppressed ; it freed from chains and bonds ; it awoke in hearts life-giving emotions ; it opened the way to the flight of reason. Had there not been this veritably creative factor in life—there would have been no history. History is the tale of the winning of freedom, the story of the triumph of Good and of Reason over Evil and Insanity.'

' And you know, I suppose, for a dead cert, that Evil and Insanity are vanquished ? ' put in the gremille mockingly.

' They are not vanquished yet, but they will be : I

assure you of that. And again I will refer to History. Compare what is with what used to be, and you will, without difficulty, agree with me, that not only the outward forms of Evil have been softened, but its actual sum has greatly diminished. Just take our fish tribe. In old days they used to catch us at any time, and especially in time of migration, when we would crazily go bang into the nets ourselves, but nowadays it's admitted that just at migration-time it's not right to catch us. Before, they used to destroy us by every sort of means. In the Urals, I have heard tell, when they harpooned fish, the water used to be red with blood for miles, but now—it's not so. Draw-nets, bow-nets, and fishing-rods—nothing else ! Why, they even discuss it in committees—what kind of nets, on what occasion, for what purpose.'

' And I suppose it's not a matter of indifference to you by what method you get into fish broth ? '

' What fish broth ? ' asked the carp wonderingly.

' Oh, go to the devil ! Called a carp and never heard of fish broth ! After that, what right have you to be talking to me ? To discuss and to defend opinion, one must at any rate first acquaint oneself with the circumstances of the case. What are you talking about if you don't know that each carp has a fish broth predestined for him ? Out of the way now or I'll run you through !'

The gremille raised his spikes, and the carp, as rapidly as his clumsiness allowed, went to the bottom. But in a few days the friends and opponents met again and began a fresh discussion.

'The other day the pike looked into our creek,' announced the gremille.

'The one you were mentioning the other day?'

'The same. He swam up and looked in, said, "It's mighty quiet along here. There must surely be some carp living here . . ."—and went off with that.'

'What am I to do then?'

'Be ready, that's all. When he comes again and fixes you with his great eyes, you just press your scales and fins down nice and flat and walk straight down his gullet.'

'Why should I? If I had been guilty of anything . . .'

'You're stupid—that's what you're guilty of. And fat, moreover. And the stupid and the fat the law commands to walk straight down a pike's gullet.'

'It's impossible that there should be such a law,' the carp exclaimed with genuine indignation. 'And the pike has no right just to swallow me like that, and must first demand an explanation. Well, I'll explain to him. I'll tell him the whole truth. I'll make him sweat seven times over with the truth.'

'I told you you were a dolt, and I say it again, "dolt, dolt, dolt!"'

The gremille finally lost his temper and gave his word in future to abstain from all intercourse with the carp. But in a few days habit got the better of him.

'Now if only all the fishes agreed together . . .' began the carp enigmatically.

But at this even the gremille got into a bit of a funk.

' What on earth is the dolt beginning to talk about now ? ' he thought. ' He 'll go letting something out, and here 's the pollard hanging about not far off. There he is looking the other way as if this were none of his business, and you may be sure he 's listening his hardest.'

' Now don't you say out every word that comes into your head ! ' he advised the carp. ' There 's no need to stretch your jaw like that. You can say what is necessary in a whisper.'

' I don't want to whisper,' the carp continued imperturbably, ' but I say quite openly that if all the fishes agree together, then . . .'

But here the gremille rudely interrupted his friend.

' Oh, one can't talk to you except with one's mouth full of peas,' he shouted at the carp, and made off home as fast as he could.

He was both annoyed at the carp and sorry for him. Although he was stupid, yet still he was the only creature one could talk frankly with. ' He won't blab to any one, he won't give one away—and in whom will you find such qualities nowadays ? It 's a poor weak sort of time now—you can't trust your own mother and father. The dace now, even if you haven't said anything bad about her herself, is quite likely, though she doesn't understand anything, to go and let it out ! And as for pollard, roach, tench, and such riff-raff, it goes without saying. For a worm they are ready to take their oath in Church.'

' Just look at yourself,' he said to the carp. ' What

71

sort of a fight could you put up if occasion demanded ? You 've got a big belly, a small head, no use for thinking with, a tiny mouth. Even the scales on you are not what you might call proper serious scales at all. There 's no dissemblance in you, no agility—a regular lump, that 's what you are ! Any creature that wants to, can just come up and eat you.'

' But what should they eat me for if I have committed no fault ? ' said the carp stubbornly as before.

' Listen, son of a fool ! Is one eaten for having done something ? Is one eaten to be punished ? One 's eaten because somebody is hungry—that 's all. You eat too, don't you ? You don't burrow in the mud with your nose for nothing, and get shellfish up. Those shellfish want to live, but you, simpleton, fill your belly with them from morning till night. Tell me, what fault have *they* committed that you punish them every minute ? Do you remember how you said the other day, " If only all the fishes agreed together . . ." ? And what if all the shellfish agreed together—you 'd have a merry time of it then, eh, simpleton ? '

The question was so directly and so unpleasantly put that the carp was confused and even blushed a little.

' But shellfish—that 's . . .' he muttered abashed.

' Shellfish are shellfish and carp are carp. Shellfish are food for carp, and carp are food for pike. And shellfish are not guilty and carp are not guilty, but both the one and the other must suffer. You can think of it for a hundred years and not think out anything different.'

After these words of the gremille's, the carp hid himself deep down in the mud and began to think at leisure. He thought and thought, and in the meantime he ate and ate shellfish. And the more he ate the more he wanted. At last, however, he thought it out.

' I don't eat shellfish because they are guilty—you were right in this,' he explained to the gremille. ' I eat them because they, these shellfish, have been provided for me by Nature herself for food.'

' Who told you that ? '

' Nobody told me, I came to this conclusion myself— from personal observation. The shellfish hasn't a soul —only a mist ; you eat shellfish and it doesn't understand. And it 's constructed so that you can't help but swallow it. You draw in water with your mouth and straight away your throat is chockfull of shellfish. I don't catch them. They swarm into my mouth of themselves. But a carp—that 's quite different. There are carp ten inches long, my boy. A creature like that you 've got to talk to before you eat him. He must have done something very shady . . . of course in *that* case . . .'

' You wait till a pike swallows you, you 'll know what you must have done then. And till then you 'd much best hold your tongue.'

' No, I won't hold my tongue. Though I 've never in my life seen a pike, I judge from what I have heard of them that they are not deaf to the voice of truth. Good gracious—can you really believe such a wickedness should be ! A carp lying there, quietly, doing no harm to anybody, and suddenly, goodness knows why, for no

73

fault of his own—he is in the pike's belly ! I shall never in life believe it ! '

' You rum 'un ! Why, a few days ago, before your very eyes, a monk took two netfuls of you fellows from the creek . . . did he catch them to look at, do you suppose ? '

' I don't know. But it 's by no means certain what has become of those carp : they might have been eaten, and they might have been put into the monks' pond —and there they are, living in luxury at the monks' expense ! '

' Oh, go along and live there too ! '

Day after day passed, and the dispute between the friends showed no signs of coming to an end. It was a quiet spot they lived in, covered with green slime, the very place for discussions. Whatever you liked to chat about, whatever fancies you indulged in—you had complete immunity. This heartened the carp so much that with each séance his excursions into the empyrean rose higher and higher.

' Fishes ought to love one another ! ' he said oratorically, ' they should each stand for all, and all for each :— that 's when veritable harmony will be effected.'

' I should like to see you approach the pike with this love of yours ! ' the gremille answered chillingly.

' I *will* approach him,' insisted the carp. ' I know words the power of which will turn any pike, when he hears them, into a carp ! '

' Let 's hear them.'

' I shall simply ask : do you know, Pike, what *virtue*

74

is and what duties it imposes upon one with regard to one's neighbour ? '

' You have put a poser this time ! Shall I run you through the belly with my spike ? '

' I do beg you not to make a joke of this.'

And again. ' We fishes will only become aware of our rights when we shall have been brought up to feelings of citizenship from our earliest years ! '

' And what the devil do you want with feelings of citizenship, pray ? '

' Oh, well . . .'

' That 's just it—" Oh, well." Feelings of citizenship are of use only where there 's place for them. What use do you suppose you 'll have for them, lying in the mud ? '

' Not in the mud—but generally speaking.'

' For instance ? '

' For instance, if a monk wants to make me into fish broth, I 'll say to him : " Thou hast no right, Reverend Father, to subject me to this fearful punishment without trial ! " '

' And he, for your rudeness, will pop you on to a frying pan, or on to hot ashes. . . . No, my friend—if you live in the mud it 's not a citizen's feelings you need, it 's a lump's—and that 's the truth. Dig yourself safely in where it 's thickest and hold your tongue ! '

Or again. ' Fishes ought not to live on fishes,' the carp raved as in a dream. ' Nature has provided lots and lots of the most delicious dishes to sustain the fish without its having recourse to this. Shellfish, flies, worms,

spiders, water-fleas ; and finally, crabs, snakes, frogs.
And all that is our property—for our use.'

' And for the use of pike there are carp,' put in the
gremille soberingly.

' No, a carp is his own property. If Nature has not
endowed him with weapons of defence as it has you for
instance, that only means that there should be a special
law made for the protection of his person.'

' What if this law is not obeyed ? '

' Then there should be published a reprimand to say :
it 's better not to make laws at all than that they should
not be obeyed.'

' And that 'll be all right, eh ? '

' I think that many will be shamed.'

Well, day after day passed and the carp raved as if he
were talking in his sleep. Another would have been
cuffed over the head for it—but he went scot-free. And
he could have havered on like this till doomsday if he
had been the least bit careful. But his dreams and
fancies so went to his head that he lost all sense. His
talk got loftier and loftier, and freer and freer—till at last
the pollard came to him with a message : ' To-morrow
the pike condescends to come to the creek, so mind you,
carp—at earliest dawn you 're to appear and report.'

The carp, however, was not afraid. For one thing he
had heard so much about the pike that he wished to
make his acquaintance; for another, he knew that he had
such a magic word that its mention would immediately
turn the fiercest pike into a carp. He had great hopes
of that word.

76

Even the gremille, seeing this faith, began to wonder whether he had not gone too far in negation. Perhaps in truth the pike is only waiting to be loved, to be counselled, to have his heart and mind enlightened. Perhaps he is really . . . kind ?

And perhaps, after all, the carp is not the ninny he seems, but on the contrary plans his career with minute calculation. Now to-morrow he will appear before the pike and just plank out the real truth to him, which he has never in all his life heard before. And the pike will go and say, ' For having told me the real truth, carp, I will give you this creek : you shall have command over it ! '

The next morning the pike came—graciousness itself. The carp looked at him and marvelled : what calumnies people had told him of the pike !—and here he was just a fish like any other. Only his mouth reached to his ears, and his gullet was just the size for the carp to go down.

' I have heard, carp,' said the pike graciously, ' that you are very wise and a past master at discussion. I should like to have a debate with you. Begin.'

' It's of happiness that I think mostly,' the carp answered modestly, but with self-respect. ' Not only happiness for myself, but for all—that all fishes should be free to swim about in all waters, and if any should want to hide in the mud, that they should be able so to do.'

' Hm ! . . . so you think that is possible ? '

' I not only think so, but I do hourly expect it.'

77

' For instance : I am swimming along and beside me
—a carp ? '

' Why not ? '

' The first time I hear of such a thing. And if I turn
round and . . . eat that carp ? '

' There isn't such a law, your Excellency ; the law
says clearly : shellfish, gnats, flies, and midges shall
serve fishes for food. And moreover, by various later
edicts thereto are added : water-fleas, spiders, worms,
beetles, frogs, and other such inhabitants of the water.
But not fishes.'

' That 's rather little for me. Pollard, is there really
such a law ? ' the pike asked, turning to the pollard.

' Obsolete, your Excellency ! ' the pollard cleverly
got out of it.

' There, I knew there couldn't be such a law. Well,
and what else, carp, do you hourly expect ? '

' I expect also that justice will be triumphant. The
strong will not oppress the weak, nor the rich the poor.
You, pike, are the strongest and ablest of all—so you
will take on yourself the hardest task, and to me, the
carp, in accordance with my humble abilities, will be
assigned some humble task. Each for all and all for
each—that 's how it will be. When we stand for each
other, no one can harm us. No sooner shall we see a net
in the distance than off we shall make ! Some under a
stone, some to the very bottom into the mud, some into
a hole or under a tree root. Fish broth will have to be
given up probably ! '

' I don't know. People are not very keen on giving

up what is good to eat. But anyway, goodness knows
when that will be. But look here : according to you I
shall have to work too ? '

' You, like the rest.'

' The first time I 've heard of such a thing. You go
and wake up, my friend.'

Whether he had slept his wits away I do not know, but
at any rate the carp had not acquired any more. At
midday he arrived again for the discussion, and not only
without the least fear, but more cheerful than ever.

' Then you think I am going to work, and you are
going to reap the benefit of my labours ? ' the pike put
him a direct question.

' . . . All will benefit from each other . . . from the
common mutual labours. . . .'

' I understand . . . from each other . . . and from *me*
too, amongst others . . . hm ! It seems to me, however,
that it 's disgraceful talk you are indulging in. Pollard,
what is this kind of talk called nowadays ? '

' Sowsh'lism, your gracious Highness ! '

' I knew it ! I 've been hearing this long time that
the carp makes seditious speeches ! I thought I 'd just
go and hear for myself. . . . So *that 's* what you are ! '

Uttering this, the pike lashed the water with his tail
in such an expressive way that, simple as the carp was,
even he understood.

' I don't mean anything, your Excellency,' he muttered in confusion. ' It 's just my simplicity. . . .'

' All right ! Simplicity is worse than thieving, they
say. If we were to give rope to the fools they would

exterminate the wise folk. I have heard a heap about you—and here you are a carp like any other. I haven't talked to you five minutes, and you 've bored me to death.'

The pike fell into a reverie and looked at the carp with so enigmatic a glance that he now quite understood. But the pike could not have been hungry, having had an immense feed the day before, for he yawned and instantly fell asleep.

But this time the carp was not so fortunate. Directly the pike finished speaking, he was surrounded by pollards and put under arrest.

In the evening, hardly had the sun set, when the carp for the third time arrived for a discussion with the pike. But now he arrived under guard, and moreover with certain injuries ; namely, the perch, when conducting the interrogation, had bitten his back, and part of his tail.

But he still heartened himself, because he had the magic word.

'Although you are my opponent,' the pike began again first, ' such is my misfortune, I do love a discussion. Go ahead, begin ! '

At these words the carp felt his heart burn within him. In a moment he drew in his stomach, quivered, lashed the water with the remains of his tail, and looking the pike straight in the eyes, cried with all his might :

' Do you know what *virtue* is ? '

The pike's mouth fell open with amazement. Mechanically he drew in the water, and with no wish to swallow the carp, just—drank him down.

The fishes who witnessed this event, for a moment stayed motionless with stupefaction, but instantly recovered and hastened to the pike—to enquire if he had graciously enjoyed his supper. And the gremille, who had already foreseen and foretold it all, swam forward and solemnly uttered the words :

' *That 's* what our discussions come to ! '

FAITHFUL TRÉSOR

OLD Trésor was watchdog to the grain-store owned by Vorotílov, a trader of the second guild in Moscow, and he watched his master's goods with a tireless eye. Never did he leave his kennel; he had never even probably seen Fleece Street, where the store was; morning till evening he just leapt at the end of his chain, barking and barking. *Caveant consules !*

And a wise creature he was. He never barked at his own people—always at strangers. If the coachman came by to steal oats—old Trésor would wag his tail: it's not much the coachman wants. But if a stranger happened to pass by on his own business, and Trésor heard him, it would be ' Help, help, stop thief ! '

The trader Vorotílov, observing Trésor's services, would say, ' That old dog is worth his weight in gold.' And if he happened to pass Trésor's kennel on his way to the grain-store, he would always say, ' Give old Trésor some dishwater.' And old Trésor would be nearly bursting with joy : ' Happy to serve you, your Excellency ! Haam, haam ! Pleasant dreams, your Excellency, haam . . . aam . . . aam ! '

Once it happened that the police inspector himself graciously came into Vorotílov's yard, and even to him old Trésor took exception. Such a din he set up, that the master, the mistress, and the children all ran out—thought it was burglars, and lo and behold, it was an honoured guest !

' Your Worship ! Pray come in, your Worship.
Down, Trésor ! What are you thinking of, you idiot,
didn't you recognise our guest ? A little vodka, your
Worship—a little something to eat ? '

' Thank you. An excellent dog this of yours, Nikanòr
Semènovitch. A well-intentioned dog ! '

' Oh, such a splendid dog ; such a splendid dog ! A
man often does not understand as well as he does.'

' He honours property, evidently, and that is rare and
pleasant to meet in these days ! ' And then, turning to
Trésor, graciously added :

' Bark, bark, my friend. Nowadays even a man, if he
wants to be well thought of, even he has to bark like
a dog ! '

Three times Vorotìlov put Trésor on trial before en-
trusting him with guarding his entire property. He
dressed himself up as a thief (it 's extraordinary how
well the dress became him), chose a nice dark night, and
went to the grain-barn to thieve. The first time he took
a crust of bread, thinking to tempt the dog with it, but
Trésor sniffed at it, and suddenly fastened on his calf !
The second time he threw him a whole sausage, ' Here,
Trésor, old man, here then ! ' but Trésor tore his coat-
tail off. The third time he took a greasy bank-note,
thought money would tempt him, but Trésor, not to be
taken in, raised such a racket that all the dogs of the
neighbourhood came running in : they stood there and
wondered why on earth the dog was barking at his
own master.

Then the merchant Vorotìlov gathered all his household together, and said to Trésor before them all : ' My entire belongings, Trésor, I commit to your care ; my wife and my children, and my goods—guard them ! Bring Trésor some dishwater ! '

Whether old Trésor understood his master's praise, or whether from the doggy nature of him, barking just burst out of his body like noise from an empty barrel—but from that day he got more and more doggish.

One eye of his would be asleep, the other looking to see if any one was getting in under the gate.   When he was tired, he would lie down, but clank his chain still : ' Here I am ! '   If they forgot to feed him, he was very glad—why, if you feed a dog every day in the week, he might cease to be like a dog at all.   If they rewarded him with kicks, he would see even in this a useful warning—for if you don't beat a dog, why, he might forget his master.

' With us dogs,' he used to say, ' you mustn't monkey about.   Beat us for a reason, beat us without reason—it 'll be a lesson to us !   Then only we 'll be real, proper dogs.'

In a word, he was a dog of principle, and his standard was so high that other dogs would look and look at him, and then just tuck in their tails—what 's the use of trying to compete ?

Fond as he was of children, even their blandishments could not move him.   The master's children would run up : ' Come for a walk with us, Trésor dear.'

' I can't.'

' Daren't you ? '

' It 's not that I daren't, I 've not the right.'

' Come on, old silly. We 'll take you so that they won't know . . . nobody will see. . . .'

' And my conscience ? '

Trésor would put his tail between his legs and hide in the kennel—away from temptation.

Many a time the thieves, too, put their heads together, ' Let us present Trésor with an album of views of the Moskva river,' but not even by this was he tempted.

' I have no need of any views,' said he ; ' in this yard I was born, in this yard I 'll lay my old bones—what views do I need ? Go away, lest you fall into temptation.'

Only one weakness Trésor had : he loved Koùtka tremendously, but even that not all the time—only now and then.

Koùtka lived in the same yard and was a nice creature too, only she had no principles. She would bark and leave off. For this reason she was not kept on a chain, but mostly near the kitchen, and went about with the children. Many delicious morsels had she eaten in her life, and never shared one with Trésor ; but Trésor bore her no grudge for that : being a lady it was only right she should have nice things. But when Koùtka's heart used to wake, she would give soft little squeals and scratch at the kitchen door.

Hearing those soft yelps, Trésor for his part used to raise such a special din that the master, understanding its meaning, himself hastened to the aid of his property. Trésor was let off his chain, and Nikìta, the yard man, took his place. And Koùtka and Trésor, agitated and happy, would run off towards the toll gate.

On these days Vorotìlov used to get as cross as two sticks, and when Trésor came back from his excursion in the early morning, the master used to beat him mercilessly with a whip. And Trésor used evidently to understand his guilt, for he did not come up to his master jauntily, like an official who has done his duty, but with his tail between his legs, humbly crawling on his stomach ; and did not howl under the blows, but squealed softly. ' Mea culpa ! mea maxima culpa ! ' In reality he was too intelligent not to understand that his master in doing this was failing to take into consideration certain extenuating circumstances ; however, he used logically to come to the conclusion that if at these times he was not beaten he would cease to be dog-like.

But what was especially valuable in Trésor was his complete lack of ambition. I do not know whether he was aware of the existence of holidays, and that it was the custom of merchants to give their faithful servants presents on those days, whether it was St. Nikanòr's day (*His* saint's day), St. Anfìsa's (*Her* day), Trésor kept jumping about on the end of his chain just the same.

' Will you be quiet, you old wretch ! ' Anfìsa Kàrpovna would call out. ' Don't you know what day it is ? '

' Never mind ! Let him bark. He is wishing us the compliments of the season ! ' Nikanòr Semènovitch would reply jokingly. ' Bark, Trésor, old man, bark ! '

Only once something like ambition awoke in him, and that was when the bad-tempered cow Ròkhla, at the request of the cowherd, had a bell hung round her neck.

To tell the truth, he was really envious when she went tinkling about the yard.

' What happiness for you, and what have you done to deserve it, after all ? ' he said to Ròkhla bitterly. ' All your service is that they milk half a pailful a day out of you, and when you come to think of it, what service is that ? You get your milk free. It doesn't depend on you : if you are fed well you give a lot of milk, if you were badly fed you would stop giving milk. You don't do a hoof's turn to serve your master, and yet look how you are rewarded ! While I, day in and day out, all on my own, *motu proprio*, am perpetually at it. No time to eat or sleep properly, gone hoarse from the trouble I have, and do you think they as much as throw a rattle to me to say, " There, old Trésor, know that we are aware of your services " ? '

' And what about your chain ? ' Ròkhla had wit enough to answer.

' Chain ? '

Only then did he understand. Up till that moment he had thought that a chain was a chain, and here, it was something like a freemason's badge. He had already been rewarded when he had not as yet deserved anything. And henceforth he had only one thing left to wish for : that they would take off his old rusty chain (he had broken it once) and give him a new strong one.

It seemed as if the merchant Vorotilov must have heard his modestly-ambitious aspiration : just before old Trésor's birthday he bought a perfectly new, beautifully wrought chain and fastened it, for a surprise, to Trésor's collar : ' Bark, Trésor, bark ! '

And he broke into the good-natured, continuous bark of dogs whose happiness is indivisible from the safety of the barn entrusted to them by the master's hand.

On the whole, old Trésor lived very well, although now and again of course there were vexations. In the world of dogs as that of men, flattery, self-seeking, and envy often play parts which are not theirs by right. There were times when even old Trésor felt the pangs of envy, but he was strong in the sense of duty done and feared nothing. This was not conceit. On the contrary, he would have been the first to give place to any new dog who proved his superiority in being invincible. Indeed he often thought with concern of who could take his place when old age had come upon him. Alas, in all the crowd of small-minded, vociferous dogs who inhabited Fleece Street, he could not find one to whom he could in honour point as his successor. So that when intrigue sought by all means to lower Trésor in his master's estimation, all it succeeded in doing—a result as surprising as it was mortifying—was to demonstrate the wholesale deterioration of doggy talents.

Once or twice envious dogs singly and in small packs had gathered in Vorotilov's yard and called upon Trésor to try his strength in competition. Then rose an unimaginable howling and yelping which filled the whole household with dismay, but to which the master listened with interest, for he understood that the time was approaching when Trésor would need a helper. In this terrific choir stood out some passable voices, but of one which gave you a sudden pain in the stomach from terror there was not a sign. A dog here and there would show considerable ability, but always he would bark too much, or else too little. During these competitions Trésor generally stopped barking, but in the end could never hold out, and to the general yelping, every note of which spoke of unnatural strain, would add his own ringing, well-modulated voice. This voice immediately removed all doubt. Hearing it, the cook used to run out of the kitchen and throw boiling water at the instigators of the intrigue. And for Trésor she would bring some dishwater.

Nevertheless the trader Vorotilov was right when he averred that nothing under the sun lasted for ever. One morning Vorotilov's assistant, passing the dog-kennel on his way to the granary, saw old Trésor asleep. Never had such a thing happened before. Whether he ever slept—probably he did—no one knew. At any rate, no one had ever come upon him asleep. Naturally the assistant was not long in letting his master know of this occurrence.

The merchant Vorotilov came out himself to old Trésor, looked at him, and seeing that he wagged his tail penitently as if to say, ' Can't understand myself how such a thing could have happened to me ! ' without anger, in a voice full of concern, said, ' Well, old man, time for the kitchen, eh ? Aged and infirm is it ? All right. You can serve me in the kitchen too.'

For the present, however, it was decided just to find Trésor a helper. It was not an easy task. Nevertheless, after considerable trouble, they succeeded in finding near the Kalougsky gates a certain Aràpka, whose reputation was already established pretty firmly.

I will not describe how Aràpka was the first to acknowledge old Trésor's authority, how implicitly he obeyed him, what great friends they became, how Trésor in the course of time was finally transferred to the kitchen, and how in spite of that he used to run out to Aràpka and disinterestedly teach him the ways of a proper watchdog to a trader. I shall only say that neither leisure nor the abundance of dainty morsels nor Koùtka's near presence ever made Trésor forget the inspired moments he spent at the end of his chain, sitting shivering from cold the long winter nights through.

Time passed, however, and Trésor grew older and older. On his throat formed a growth which bent his head down towards the ground, so that he could rise to his feet only with difficulty ; his eyes were almost sightless, his ears hung limp, his coat was matted and came out in handfuls, his appetite was gone, and as he was always cold now, he squeezed himself as close to the stove as he could.

' Say what you like, Nikanòr Semènovitch, but old Trésor is getting all mangy now,' the cook announced to Vorotìlov once.

This time the merchant said not a word. But the

cook would not leave off, and in a week announced once more : ' I am afraid for the children catching something from old Trésor. He is very mangy now.'

But even then Vorotìlov said nothing. Then in two days the cook came running in in a great rage, and cried that she would not stop another minute if old Trésor was not taken away. And as the cook was a great dab at preparing sucking-pig with buckwheat, and Vorotìlov loved this dish to distraction, Trésor's fate was sealed.

' It's not for such a fate that I took the trouble to train old Trésor,' said Vorotìlov with feeling, ' but evidently the proverb says rightly, " For a dog—a dog's death." . . . Drown old Trésor ! '

And so they led old Trésor out into the yard. All the household came out to look at the faithful dog's death-agony ; even the children ran to the windows. Aràpka was there too and, seeing his old teacher, affectionately wagged his tail. Trésor was so old that his legs could scarcely carry him, and evidently he did not understand ; but when he got to the gate, his strength left him, and they had to drag him along by the scruff of his neck.

Of what happened then, history is silent, but old Trésor did not come back.

And soon Aràpka finally erased Trésor's image from Vorotìlov's heart.

THE LIBERAL

In a certain country once upon a time there lived a Liberal, and so frank he was, that he used before any one uttered a word to cry loudly, ' Gentlemen, gentlemen, what are you doing ? You are laying up trouble for yourselves ! ' And no one was angry with him, but on the contrary every one said, ' Let him warn us—it 's good for us ! '

' Three factors,' he used to say, ' must enter into the basis of every social organisation : freedom, security, and activity. If society is deprived of freedom it lives without ideals, without vigour of thought, lacking the basis for creative work or faith in its future. If society feels that it has no security, this sets upon it the seal of low-spiritedness and renders it indifferent to its own fate. If society is deprived of the possibility of activity it becomes incapable of spontaneous effort, of managing its affairs, and little by little even loses the idea of the State.'

Thus the Liberal reasoned, and to tell the truth, reasoned correctly. He saw that all round him men went about like autumn flies, and said to himself, ' That is because they do not regard themselves as the builders of their fate. They are like so many convicts, to whom good fortune or bad comes without any forethought on their part, who do not give themselves up care-free to their sensations, because they cannot tell whether these are really sensations or some extravagant fancy.' In a word, the Liberal was firmly convinced that only the above-mentioned three factors can give society a stable basis, and bring with them all the other blessings necessary for the development of the social organism.

But this was by no means all : the Liberal not only reasoned in a high-minded manner, but also burned to do good works. His dearest wish was that the ray of light which lit his reason should also pierce the surrounding gloom, illuminate it, and fill all living creatures with loving-kindness. He held all men to be his brothers, and called on all to taste of the sweets of wisdom beneath the shelter of the ideals he held dear.

Although this aspiration to bring his ideals from the empyrean to the field of actuality did smack of something politically dangerous, the Liberal glowed with such sincerity of zeal, and moreover was such a dear and so nice to every one, that he was forgiven even for being politically unsound. He knew how to vindicate truth with a smile, could, when necessary, play the simpleton, and could show off his disinterestedness to advantage. But chiefly he never demanded anything at the point of the sword, but always only *within the limits of possibility*.

Of course the expression ' within the limits of possibility' was not particularly attractive to his zeal; but the Liberal accepted it in the first place for the sake of the common good, which with him always stood first, and secondly, in order to guard his ideals from an untimely death. Moreover, he knew that the ideals actuating him were too abstract in character to have a direct influence on life. What is freedom? security? activity? These were all abstract terms which had undoubtedly to be given a practical form before they could result in the flowering of society.

These terms, abstract as they were, could educate society, could raise the level of its faith and hopes, but to bring a tangible good, which should give a feeling of actual well-being, they could not. In order to reach this good, in order to make the ideal accessible to all, it was necessary to have them in small change as it were, and in this form only to put them to the purpose of healing the ills which beset mankind. It is in this process of converting it into small change that the expression ' as far as possible ' comes spontaneously into existence—from two sources : one which forced him *in a certain measure* to forgo exclusiveness, the other which obliged him *to a certain extent* to curtail his ideals.

Our Liberal understood all this perfectly, and arming himself with these reflections, he girded himself for the battle with actuality. And first of all, of course, he addressed himself to the Well-Informed.

' Freedom—there is nothing prejudicial in that, I think ? ' he asked them.

' Not only is there nothing prejudicial, but on the contrary it is most praiseworthy,' answered the Well-Informed : ' it is only a calumny against us that we do not desire freedom : in reality it is the one thing we hanker for. . . . But of course, within limits. . . .'

' Hm . . . within limits. . . . I understand. And what about security ? '

' Very laudable too. Of course also within limits.'

'And what do you think of my ideal of social activity ? '

'The very thing we have been needing. But naturally within limits too.'

Well, if it was to be within limits, well and good ! The Liberal himself understood well enough that it could not be otherwise. Let a colt out without a bridle, he will in one moment do as much damage as you cannot mend in a year ! But bridled—it's work with a blessing on it ! The colt goes along, keeps looking back —' I 'll just give it you with a whip, you colt . . . there ! '

And so the Liberal began taking action—' within limits ' : cut a bit there, snip off a trifle there, and in a third place he would make himself scarce altogether. And the Well-Informed looked on and rejoiced. At one time they were so carried away by his work that you might have thought they had become Liberals themselves.

'Continue,' they encouraged him, ' go round it here, soften it there, and over here do not touch it at all. And all will be well. We, my dear friend, would gladly have let you, the goat, come into our garden—but you see what a hedge there is round it ! '

'I see, yes, I see,' the Liberal agreed, ' only I am ashamed of destroying my ideals—oh, so ashamed ! '

'Well, be ashamed a little : shame will not eat your eyes out ! But *within the limits of possibility* you will carry out your project ! '

However, as the project did *within the limits of possibility* little by little near its realisation, the Well-Informed began to be aware that even in this form the Liberal's ideals did not smell of roses. On the one hand, the conception was too wide, on the other, the time was not ripe—minds were not ready for its assimilation.

' They 're too much for us, your ideals,' said the Well-Informed to the Liberal, ' we are not ready for them—we 'll never hold out ! '

And they reckoned up all their irresponsibilities and their basenesses so minutely and so clearly that the Liberal had perforce to agree that there was some fatal flaw in his enterprise—get into its trousers it would not, and that was all about it.

' Oh, how distressing it is ! ' he said reproachfully to Fate.

' How odd you are ! ' the Well-Informed returned comfortingly, ' there is nothing to cry about. What do you want ? To ensure a future for your ideals ?—but we are not opposing that. Only don't be in such a dreadful hurry ! If you cannot get it *within the limits of possibility*, be content that you will win *at any rate something*. Even this *at any rate something* has its value. Little by little, and gradually, without hurry, after due prayer to God—and presently you find you have one foot in the temple ! No one has as much as looked into the temple since it was built ; and here you 've been and looked in . . . Thank your stars for that anyway.'

Well, there was nothing to be done, he had to be content with that. If one could get nothing *as far as possible*, one would have to snatch *at any rate something* and say thank you. So the Liberal did, and soon got so used to his new position that he wondered himself how he could have been so stupid as to think any other limit possible. All sorts of parallels came to his aid too. For instance—even the millet-seed will not yield grain immediately, but only in due course. First you have to put it into the ground, then to wait while the process of germination occurs in it. Then it will put up a shoot, which will sprout, make leaves, then an ear, and so on. See through how many wonders the seed must pass before it gives a hundredfold ! So it would be in the effort after ideals. You put *at any rate something* into the earth—then sit and wait.

And so it was. The Liberal put *at any rate something* into the ground, and sat and waited. He waited and waited, but not a sign of sprouting did *at any rate something* give. Whether it fell on stony ground or rotted on a piece of manure—just you try and make it out !

' What can the reason be ? ' murmured the Liberal in consternation.

' The reason is that you over-reach yourself,' the Well-Informed answered. ' And ours is a poor, weak, mean-souled people. You go to it with a gift of food, and it tries to drown you in a spoon. One must have real knack to keep oneself unspotted with a people like that ! '

' Good gracious ! what is the use of talking about being unspotted at this point ! I was not over-clean when I started, but now precious little have I left un-spotted. At first I went to work *within the limits of possibility*, then I moved on to *at any rate something—* can one go downhill farther ? '

' Of course one can. Wouldn't you like, for instance, to work by adjustment to rascality ? '

' How do you mean ? '

' It 's very simple. You say you have brought us ideals, and we say " very nice " ; but if you want us to enter into it feelingly you must be adaptable. And later, possibly we too, if we see it serves a useful purpose, may . . . We have seen a thing or two, my dear sir, we have met these idealists before. The other day General Crocodilov presented himself just like this too. " Gentlemen," he says, " my ideal is the lock-up !—walk in ! " We went and believed him, and now there we are, under lock and key.'

The Liberal mused deeply when he heard these words. There was nothing left of his ideals except their labels anyway, and here he was recommended actual baseness for them ! That way, before you turn round you 'll be a skunk yourself ! God give him counsel !

And the Well-Informed, seeing his reflectiveness, began to egg him on, ' You 've begun it, Liberal, you must now put it through ! You stirred us up, you must satisfy us now. . . . Take action ! '

So he began taking action. And all by adjustment to rascality. He would try now and again to slip off to the side, and the Well-Informed would instantly pluck him by the sleeve. ' Why are you looking aside, Liberal ?—eyes front ! '

In this way, day after day passed, and with them came

nearer the day of success. Of ideals there was left not a trace—nothing but sheer abomination; but the Liberal was still not downhearted. 'What matter if I have plunged my ideals up to the ears in mud ? Yet I myself stand firm as a rock and unharmed ! To-day I roll about in the mud, but to-morrow the sun will come out, dry the mud—and I shall be gay and dandy as ever !' And the Well-Informed, hearing his boasts, said in chorus, 'Exactly so !'

And as he was walking in the street with a friend one day, chatting about ideals as usual, and praising his wisdom, suddenly he felt something wet splashing his cheek a little. Where had it come from ? what was it ? The Liberal looked up : was it raining by any chance ? But he saw that there was not a cloud in the sky and the sun was shining away overhead like blazes. Although there was a breeze, there were no regulations that slops should be emptied out of windows, so one could not suspect this operation.

'What an extraordinary thing !' the Liberal said to his friend : 'there 's no rain, there are no slops, and yet I 've wet on my cheek !'

'Do you see a man lurking round the corner there ?' returned the friend. 'He did it ! He wanted to spit at you for your Liberal doings, but he had not the courage to do it straight in your face. So he, "by adjustment to rascality," spat from round the corner, and the wind brought it you.'

THE POOR WOLF

THE rabbit once got into trouble with the wolf. Another beast would certainly have been touched by the rabbit's self-sacrificing spirit, would not have contented himself with a promise to pardon him, as the wolf did, but *would* have pardoned him there and then. But of all the predatory animals of the temperate and the northern climes, the wolf is the least open to the sentiment of magnanimity.

However, it is not by his own will that he is so cruel, but because he has a perverse nature—he cannot eat anything but meat. And to get meat-food he cannot do otherwise than deprive a living creature of its life. In a word, it constrains him to commit a crime—to do murder.

He does not come by his food easily. Death is not sweet to any creature, and it is just with death that he comes to every one. So the strong beasts defend themselves against him, and those who cannot stand up for themselves, others defend. Often and often the wolf goes hungry, and with sore ribs as well. At such times he sits down, lifts his muzzle, and howls so piercingly that for a verst round every living beast's heart sinks with terror and dismay. And his mate howls still more miserably, because she has cubs and there is nothing to give them to eat.

There is no animal on the face of the earth who does not hate the wolf, who does not call down curses on him.

The whole forest moans when he appears. ' Accursed wolf ! Murderer ! ' and he runs on and on, not daring to turn his head, and after him they call, ' Robber ! Torturer ! '

A month ago the wolf went off with an old peasant woman's sheep—the woman has not dried her tears yet, ' Acursed wolf ! Slaughterer ! ' And he since then has not had so much as a poppy-seed in his mouth. He ate that sheep, and could not get another kill. The peasant woman howls and he howls. . . . How can one make out the rights of it ?

They say the wolf robs the peasant, but the peasant, when he is angry, is fierce too. He beats him with a stick, he shoots him with a gun, he digs pits for him and sets traps and lays ambushes.

And if you kill him, he is no good to you. His meat is no use, his fur is coarse and doesn't warm you. The only satisfaction is sticking him alive on a pitchfork : there, let your blood, accursed beast, drip out of you, drop by drop !

The wolf cannot, without depriving others of life, himself live on the earth—that is his misfortune. But he does not understand this. He only thinks that he lives. The horse carries weights, the cow gives milk, the sheep fleece, and he—robs and kills. The horse, the cow, the sheep, the wolf, all ' live ' according to their kind.

At last, once among the wolves, there appeared one who for many years killed and robbed, and suddenly, in his old age, it began to dawn on him that there was something in his life not as it should be.

He lived, this wolf, when he was young, like a dare-devil, and was one of the few beasts of prey who scarcely ever went hungry. Night and day he robbed, and went scot-free. He used to take sheep from under the very noses of the shepherds ; in the villages he broke into the farmyards ; he killed cows ; once he bit the forester nearly to death ; he carried off into the forest a little boy under the eyes of the villagers. He heard that for these doings he was hated and accursed, but he only became fiercer and fiercer.

' They should hear what goes on in the forest,' he used to say. ' There is not a moment when there is not a murder there, when some small beast is not shrieking as it parts with its life—but what 's the sense of paying attention to that ? '

And so he lived, with his robberies, and presently reached the age when a wolf is said to be ' hardened.' He grew a bit heavy but did not leave off robbing : indeed he seemed even to have grown fiercer. But once, as luck would have it, a bear got him. And bears do not like wolves, because wolves set on them in packs, and often in the forest, so the rumour goes, in some place, Mikhaelo Ivanovitch gets the worst of it : his grey enemies have torn his fur coat into bits.

The bear held the wolf in his paws and thought, ' What am I to do with him, the villain ? If I eat him I 'll be ill ; if I strangle him and leave him, the forest will be infected with the smell of his carcase. I 'll see if he has a conscience. If he has, and swears he will not rob any more—I will let him go.'

' Wolf, I say, Wolf,' said the bear, ' haven't you got a conscience ? '

' Good gracious, your dignified Excellency,' answered the wolf, ' how is it possible to live a single day without a conscience ? '

' Evidently it is possible, since you live. I think every day of God's year we hear how you have flayed some creature or murdered it—does that look like conscience ? '

' Your dignified Excellency, allow me to make this known to you. Is it my duty to feed myself and my mate, to bring up my cubs ? What would be your judgment on this point ? '

Mikhaelo Ivanovitch thought a little ; he saw that if it was just for the wolf to live on the earth, he had a right to feed himself.

' It is your duty,' he said.

' And I can't touch anything but meat ! Now if you take yourself, your Excellency, for example. You make a nice little meal off raspberries, or take a loan of some honey off the bees, or suck a few oats, but for me these things are simply as if they didn't exist ! And then again —you have another privilege, your Excellency : in the winter, when you go to your lair, you have no need of anything except your own paw. As for me—summer and winter—there is not a moment when I do not have to think about food ! And always meat, you know. Well, how am I to get this food if I don't first kill some one ? '

The bear thought over these words ; still he wanted to try the wolf a little.

' Well,' he said, ' you might go a bit easier so to speak. . . .'

' I do, your dignified Excellency, make it as easy as I can. The fox, now, she torments ; she tears at a creature once and jumps away, and tears at it again and jumps away again. . . . But I just go at their throats—and it 's all over ! '

Still harder did the bear think. He saw that what the wolf said was dead true, and yet he was afraid to let him go : he would set to at his robber's work again.

' Repent, Wolf ! ' he said.

' I have nothing to repent of, your Excellency. No one is an enemy to his life, and I am no exception. Then what is my fault ? '

' Well, can't you promise . . . ? '

' I can't promise, your Excellency. The fox now, she would promise you anything. But I can't.'

What was to be done ? The bear thought again and made up his mind.

' You are the most unfortunate of beasts, that 's my last word to you,' he said to the wolf. ' I cannot condemn you, although I know I take much sin upon my soul by letting you go. I can only add one thing : in your place I would not only set no value on my life, but I would count death a mercy ! Just think over these words of mine.'

And he let the wolf free to the four winds of heaven.

Directly the wolf was liberated from the bear's hug, he set to at his old game. The forest groaned from his murderings. He kept going to the same village, and in

two or three nights killed off a whole flock for no purpose
—and minded not a bit. He would lie in a swamp, his
belly well filled, and stretch himself out with half-shut
eyes. He was even going to attack the bear who had
been so kind to him, but luckily the bear got to hear of
it in time and only shook his paw at him from a distance.

Well, for some time he lived this turbulent life, and at
last old age came upon him. His strength waned, his
agility left him, and a peasant man, too, injured his spine
by a blow with a log : although he got well of that, there
was little of the former dare-devil killer left in him. He
would start off in pursuit of a hare, and feel his legs
powerless. He would come to the edge of the forest
and try to steal a sheep from the flock, and the dogs
would come rushing up, barking furiously. And he
would tuck in his tail and make off empty.

' Am I even afraid of dogs now ? ' he would say to
himself.

He would come back to his lair and set to howling.
In the forest the owl sobbed and in the swamp he howled
—what a to-do there was in the village !

One day, however, he got hold of a little lamb and
began to drag him off to the forest. The lamb had no
sense yet : the wolf dragged him along and he did not
understand—only kept saying :

' What is it ?   What is it ? '

' I 'll just show you what it is . . . s-s-scoundrel ! ' said
the wolf in a rage.

' Uncle dear, I don't want to go for a walk in the
forest ! I want to go to Mammy ! I won't do it any

more, Uncle, I won't, any more!' the lamb half bleated, half sobbed, suddenly guessing. 'Oh shepherd, dear shepherd; oh doggies, doggies!'

The wolf stopped and listened. Many sheep had he killed in his time, and they all seemed indifferent somehow. Directly the wolf seized them they always just shut their eyes without moving, as if it were their natural fate. And here this baby—how he cried! he wanted to live! Oh, evidently this cursed life was sweet to every one! And he, the wolf—old, he was—old, and yet he would like to live another hundred years.

And he remembered Toptygin's [1] words, 'in your place I would count death instead of life a blessing.' Why was that? Why was it that for all the other creatures of the earth life was a blessing and *for him* it was a curse and a shame?

And without waiting for an answer he let the lamb go from his maw and went slowly, with his tail drooping, towards his lair, there to think it out at leisure.

But thinking could clear up nothing for him, except what he had known long ago—that there was no way for him, the wolf, to live, except by murder and by robbery.

He lay flat down on the ground and could not get settled anyhow. His mind told him one thing, his vitals were afire with something else. Whether it was sickness weakening him, or old age putting an end to him, whether it was hunger that had exhausted him, he could not get a hold of himself as he used to do. In his

[1] A folklore nickname for the bear.—*Tr.*

ears kept sounding, ' Accursed beast, murderer, torturer ! ' What did it matter that he did not know what
wilful sin he had committed ? That could not stop the
curses ! Oh, it was true, evidently, what the bear had
said : there was nothing for him but to do away with
himself !

Then here too was the trouble : a beast cannot even
do away with himself. He can do nothing of his own
will, a beast. It 's as though he lived in a dream, and he
dies as in a dream too. Perhaps dogs will tear him to
pieces, or a peasant shoot him, and he will give a couple
of snarls, and convulsions will seize his body for a second,
and it will be all over. And where death has come from
—he will not have guessed. He could perhaps starve
himself to death. . . . Of late he had even stopped chasing
hares, and just mooned round the birds. He would
catch a young crow or snipe, and that would have to do
for his meal. And even then the other animals used
to cry out, ' Accursed ! accursed ! accursed ! '

Verily accursed ! How can one live just in order to
kill and rob ? True that it was unjust to curse him, it
was unreasonable ; he did not do it of his free choice—
but how can they help cursing him ? How many beasts
had he done to death in his time ! How many women
and peasant men had he left with nothing, and made
them miserable for life !

Many years did he spend in the torture of these
thoughts ; only one word rang in his ears, ' Accursed,
accursed, accursed ! ' And he himself echoed oftener
and oftener, ' Verily accursed—I *am* accursed, a mur-

derer, a torturer ! ' And still, torn by hunger, he went out to hunt. He bit, tore, and killed his prey. . . .

And he began to call on death. ' Death ! Death ! Will you not free me from myself ? ' he howled, day and night, looking at the sky. And beasts and men, hearing those howls, yelled in fear, ' Murderer, murderer, murderer ! ' He could not even implore heaven without calling down curses upon him from all sides.

At last death took pity on him. There appeared in those parts some trappers, and the neighbouring squires with their help got up a hunt after the wolf. He lay there one day in his lair and heard a call. He rose and went out. He saw before him the way was marked out by stakes, and behind him and at each side peasant men watching. But he no longer attempted to break through, but walked with lowered head to meet death. . . .

And suddenly something struck him between the eyes.

' Here . . . death the deliverer ! '

AN IDLE CONVERSATION

I⊤ does not happen now, but there was a time when even among statesmen there used to be Voltairians now and again. In the highest government circles it was the fashion, and smaller officials followed suit.

At that very time there was once a Governor[1] who did not believe in many things which others in their simplicity still believed. And in particular he could not understand for what reason the post of Governor was instituted.

The Marshal of the Nobility in that province, on the other hand, believed in everything and understood the meaning of the institution of Governors to a nicety. And so once they settled down in the Governor's study and began to argue.

'Between ourselves, now,' said the Governor, 'really I do not understand. In my opinion, if all of us Governors were done away with, not a soul would notice.'

'Oh, your Excellency, what expressions you use!' the Marshal of the Nobility exclaimed in astonishment and even alarm.

'Well, of course, this is in confidence. . . . But speaking candidly, I repeat, I am completely at a loss to understand! Think of it : people live in peace, keep God in mind, honour the Tsaritsya—and suddenly—they are sent a Governor! Why? Where from? What's the reason?'

---

[1] Of a goubernia or province.—*Tr.*

' The reason is Authority,' returned the Marshal of the Nobility. ' It is impossible to do without it. At the top there is the Governor, in the middle the captain of police, at the bottom the rural constable. And at the side, so to speak, there are the Marshals, Presidents of Commissions, the military.'

' I know. But what for ? You say the rural constable—that 's the one for the peasants—I understand that too. Now just consider : the peasant lives there in his village, tills the fields, ploughs, cuts hay, increases, multiplies—in short goes through the round of his habitual life. And suddenly from goodness knows where up starts the rural constable . . . why ? What has happened ? '

' Nothing has happened, but it *may* happen, your Excellency ! '

' I don't believe it. If people live as it pleases them, what need for a constable ? If they quietly keep God in mind, honour the Tsaritsya, what could be better ? And what can the constable do ? What more can he add ? If God gives a good harvest, there will be a good harvest ; if God does not give a good harvest, they 'll manage somehow. What is there for the constable to do ? Can he make the harvest less or more by a single ear of corn ? No, he 'll rush in, make a fuss, create a disturbance, and as likely as not finish up by clapping some one in jail. That 's all.'

' Well, but the constable doesn't put him in jail for nothing. He will have done something.'

' However, you will grant that if the devil had not

brought him, all would have gone in its usual course and no " something " would have happened—at any rate nobody would have been in jail. And as soon as he appears the " something " immediately appears in his train.'

' Oh, but, your Excellency, there are constables and constables. We had one now . . .'

' No, but just hear me out. I am not speaking personally and I am not trying to show off with paradoxes to you. I speak from first-hand knowledge—from my own experience. For instance, I leave the goubernia, and what instantly happens ? I have not had time to get beyond the customs barrier [1] when suddenly there is a complete change of atmosphere over the whole goubernia—a mellifluous air. The police inspector ceases to gallop about, the district police no longer run around, the constables stop their zeal. Even the simpletons who have absolutely no idea of my existence, even they feel that some hitch has disappeared from out their lives, some hitch from which they felt a hurt on every side. What does this portent mean, I ask you ? Why this, my dear sir, this : that my substitute has not the power to do all I can, and that the lives of all officials and all the populace are eased by that much. But now I come back to my post. Noise, rattle, riding, running. . . . The man who wore a cap puts on a three-cornered hat, the man who had lived in peace and comfort the whole month once more returns to depression : all see before them the prospect of endless disgusting

[1] Customs duties were levied on country produce in towns.—*Tr.*

111

red-tape, flim-flam, and delay. . . . But why waste time in talking of it ? You must to some extent have had experience of it yourself. . . .'

The Marshal of the Nobility did indeed remember that he was not guiltless in that respect. As soon as the governor was outside the gates, ' Here—the tarantás,' [1] he used to call, and off to the country. And there he used to walk about in undress until the authorities called him to his duty. Only one formality he used to observe : passing the vice-governor's house he would come in for a minute and say :

' If anything happens, Arèfy Ivànich, you might send me down a messenger.'

' Why, what should happen ? God speed you ! '

' Well, good-bye then. My kind regards to Capitol-ina Sergéyvna. Go on, driver ! ' And that 's all they saw of him.

' Well, I have taken myself off,' he said, ' but not because of that. It 's simply that one wants a rest now and again . . . and so one takes the opportunity.'

' " Rest," there you are ! And who prevented your resting ? Is there any sin in resting ? There is not. But he prevented it simply because he is the Governor—that 's all. Now let us go a little further. Have you noticed how unofficial people talk of the Governor when they want to praise him ? " This is a good Governor," they say, " he is not active. He leaves people alone." There you are. That means that the most valuable attribute in a Governor is that he should benevolently

[1] A carriage used for long journeys.—*Tr.*

do nothing. And indeed, if you will look at it candidly, what good can his interference in the affairs of the populace conceivably do ? For one thing, he comes to the goubernia an absolute stranger. For another, he may have been taught something some time, but certainly not what is of any use. Then—he knows nothing of statistics ; of the character and customs of the people he has no notion ; where what river flows and why, he will only find out when he has driven some five times up and down the goubernia ; of railroads he only knows the times of some trains so as not to miss them, but why a line was laid, what revenue it brought in this year or that, where there is need for a branch—all this is for him wrapped in mystery. And he could find it all—the information is all at hand—but it does not interest him—it is no use. Nothing will come of getting this information.[1]

' Or what concerns commerce, trades, production : as boot-making, market-gardening : in one place they make bast mats, in another reaping-hooks—why ? How is it ? Which side 's your bread buttered ? '

' But, your Excellency ! ' interposed the Marshal when the Governor had got so worked up, ' I am a local man and even I don't know all this ! '

' You are different ; you are the Marshal. They bring you beef for dinner. It does not matter to you in the least where it comes from, so long as it 's edible. But I—the Governor—should know everything. I might be asked any day, " What is the state of market-gardening in your goubernia ? " '

[1] Of course this is only possible in a story.—*Shchedrin.*

' Yes, in these times one must be prepared for anything.'

' In these days, my dear sir, they require every kopek to be accounted for—that every mortal thing which can give revenue should be known ; would it not be useful now to levy a tax on it ? That 's how it is nowadays. So one just answers to prevent any possible trouble, " Oh, it leaves much to be desired." '

' Y-yes. And yet our cabbage . . .'

' There you are—" cabbage." And I knew of it only the other day. They bring me up a cabbage—I thought it was from Algiers—and it 's just from Posdéyevka.'

' From Posdéyevka. . . . Yes, that 's true. They have carrots and turnips—all kinds of vegetables. It 's always like that with us. We go about to different Emses and Marienbads to drink the waters, and we 've got water of our own here at Posdéyevka—and better too, for the Marienbad water upsets your stomach.'

' And tell me now, who has instituted this cabbage ? The governor ? Not much ! Our wretched little peasant, sir, some Siméon Maliaka from Posdéyevka perhaps, happening to be in Rostov, saw how they grew cabbages there, and dug himself a kitchen garden, and seeing him, others began too.'

' That is quite true, your Excellency,' the Marshal was forced to admit.

' And all our industries are carried on in that local sort of way. In one place it 's like Eden, and in the next there 's not a thing. You know, next to this Posdéyevka there is a village called Rasvalíkhina—not a trace of gardens there—but the peasants there to a man are all woolworkers. In the summer they work the land in the usual peasant manner, and in winter they all scatter and work wool. And this, too, has not been instituted by the Governor, but by an ordinary peasant—some Abramko or other has been to the Kalyazinsky ooyezd[1] and brought it from there. Now you see how it is. Cabbage, cucumber, wool, boots, bast mats . . . all this from the population ! Who do you suppose built the belfry in your Rasterayevka ? The Governor ? Why no—a trader, Poligarp Aggeev Paralychév, built it, and the Governor was only present at its consecration, and ate sturgeon and marrow pie.'

' That 's true.'

' And who instituted curing herrings at Pereslav ? '

' True again. Not the Governor.'

' And salmon from the rapids, and the morgka berry, and the sweets from Rgev and Kolomensk ? The Governor, eh ? '

' But one moment, your Excellency. After all, besides horticulture and the production of groceries, there are plenty of other things. . . .'

' Such as ? '

' Taxes, for instance. . . . Their collection, their levy. . . .'

' And what are taxes ? Have you ever heard ? '

' Taxes. . . . Well . . . they are a kind of . . . evidence of property . . .' the Marshal began, but getting mixed, stopped.

[1] District.—*Tr.*

' That 's just it—" evidence." You think it 's pleasant, this evidence ? Here he is, come for the taxes. Dear me, how delightful ! He might have brought the secret of Muramsk cucumbers or the smoking of Tambov ham—but no—it 's squeezing out taxes ! And how do you suppose I am to make this evidence of property materialise if the Posdeyevka peasants' cabbage has failed ? What is my rôle then ? I send round a circular to the captains of the police—that 's all, and the captains of the police will fill the goubernia with din, that 's all again. Anyway, I have to coerce them—to do what ? I don't know. The captain of the police makes a din—for what purpose he doesn't know either : what has happened ? where have the government taxes disappeared ? Whether a bad harvest has left the peasant destitute, or drunkenness has ruined him, or the extortioner fastened upon him, or the peasant begins to jib and put his money by in a pitcher ? How many different reasons may there be, and there is more in it still ! But we fuss and shout and will listen to nothing. Give us taxes and that 's all about it ! '

' Yes, that is quite true. They will fuss and shout and give us a taste of the birch even—and what they can get as a result they don't know themselves ! ' sadly agreed the Marshal.

The companions mused a moment.

The Marshal was the first to wake from his reverie. He did not as yet evidently despair, and the question was just rising to his lips : ' And what about the population's morality ? education ? the sciences ? the

116

arts ? ' when the Governor, evidently guessing his companion's thoughts, gave him such a severe look, that the latter could only get out : ' And the national food supply ? '

' Are you not ashamed ? ' the Governor only asked him point-blank for answer.

The Marshal blushed. He remembered how early in the year in his capacity of President of the Zemstvo Committee he travelled about the countryside. He remembered and was covered with confusion.

' But is it really . . . ? ' he exclaimed, but suddenly remembered something : ' Stay. Surely there is an object : the furthering of social unity ? '

' What social unity ? '

' Ours—of our local society.'

' Hm. . . . So you think I shall further social unity ? '

' You, and Madame, your wife . . . Loukeria Ivanovna.'

' Loukeria Ivanovna perhaps . . . but not I. . . . No —I beg you to excuse me ! Besides, who wants this social unity . . . and of this local society at that ? '

The companions were finally silent. And perhaps they would have begun to feel uncomfortable had not the cashier from the goubernia office entered just in time.

It was the thirtieth of the month. In those times, as every one knows, salaries were paid on that day, and the cashiers of all government departments used to come to the Heads with ledgers in which were written the signatures of receipt.

117

The Governor took the bundle of notes from the cashier, counted them in leisurely manner, laid them down on the table, and signed the book.

' Well, and this ? ' said the Marshal, laughing, and pointing to the bundle of notes. ' And what meaning do we attach to this ? '

' Y-yes . . . you mean . . . *this* ? ' echoed the Governor, as if just awakened.

' Yes, this. . . . Exactly. . . . Just *this*.'

' Hm ! *This* ? . . . Oh, this is . . . a reward ! '

A VILLAGE FIRE

(Maybe a tale, maybe a true story)

In the village of Sophoníha about midday a fire broke out. It happened in the very busiest time of the June ploughing. Both the men and the women were all in the fields. They say a soldier was passing through, sat down under a window, smoked his pipe, and went on. And then a fire broke out.

The village was burnt to the ground. Only a bit, the part where the barns stood, remained. In a single hour the peasants lost everything and became paupers. Old Granny Praskovya was burnt, and Petka, Tatiana's little boy. The men and women, seeing the thick smoke, ran in from the fields, leaving their ploughs and horses. But by that time there was nothing left to save. It was a good thing that the cattle were out and the manure carted, or it would have been desperate—nothing left but to die. The small children, who when the fire broke out were playing in the road, took refuge in the river, and were yelling desperately. Growing girls, with babies in their arms, gazed in terror at the charred wood of the houses and the bricks of the stoves now laid bare.

Aunt Tatiana was a widow, still young and vigorous. Some six years ago her husband had died, but she continued to work her fields. She paid the village community for half his land, ploughed, reaped, and cut the hay herself. She had an only boy, Petka, about eight

119

years old, whom she adored, and in whom she saw a
future husbandman. He himself did too. He used to
say, ' I shall be a mujik, mother—I 'll work the fields.'
The village people were all fond of him. He was a
sharp boy, and loving too, and went to school already.
He used to go through the village past the old men.
' Well, ploughman, do you help your mother ? ' they
would ask. ' I do.'

The road was being filled with all sorts of rubbish.
To a peasant everything is dear, everything of value.
The people with their families wandered each about the
ruin of his house, pulling out all they could find : an old
horse-shoe, a rusty nail, a bit of harness, a broken piece
of a plough. . . . Some people's cellars remained, but as
it was a time of Fast (the Fast of St. Peter) the cellars
were empty. An astute beggar, who had begged for
' pieces ' some ten years, ran to and fro, crying :

' Where is my pot ? [1] Where is it ? Who has gone
off with my pot ? Tell me.'

Granny Avdótya wandered up and down the street
showing every one two tickets of the lottery-loan. The
edges were burnt, but the centre, with some coupons,
was intact.

' 'Spect they 'll give it you, Mihéy,' the Elder said to
her comfortingly. ' Why, you can see the numbers
even, on these singed coupons. The barynia [2] will do
something for you in Petersburg.' [3]

---

[1] *I.e.* pot of money.— *Tr.*   [2] The lady, *i.e.* the squiress.— *Tr.*
[3] An incident from life.   In 1872 a peasant woman from the village
of Zaogerya (Ooyezd of Ooglitsk) came to see the author and showed

The old men had gathered together discussing the common calamity. All the faces were haggard with anxiety ; tears were running down some. It was agreed to go all together to a neighbouring village and beg for shelter till such time as they could knock up some kind of temporary dwellings. Then the Elder was sent off on horseback to the town to get money assistance and the insurance.

The village priest appeared, and went about among the peasants trying to comfort them.

' Who gave ? God,' he said. ' Who taketh away ? God. Do you think He does not know ? '

The peasants mutely made obeisance to him.

' And don't you be downhearted,' he continued. ' Why ? What is it ? Who allowed it ? You have your cattle, your agricultural implements are all safe, the manure is carted. What more does a husbandman need ? Perhaps the Administration will allow you money for building, the pomeshchitsa [1] will send you in some grain, and I too. Do you think I don't pray for you ? Not only for you, for *all* I pray : for all orthodox Christians. That 's how it is.'

The peasants made obeisance again, and the chatty priest went on :

him two or three tickets charred at the edges but so that the numbers on the coupons were legible. I asked some good friends to see about it at the Bank. Every one thought the case clear, but Mr. Lamansky, the then director of the Bank, judged otherwise. He deemed it impossible to reissue the tickets, or even to refund their original value. This, you understand, in the interests of the Bank. See how warmly true officials have the interests of the Treasury at heart !—*Shchedrin.*

[1] Landowner, lady.—*Tr.*

' If you keep the fear of the Lord in your hearts, and go to Church, you will see how soon He will return a hundredfold. The harvest bids fair to be good this year. The winter corn is splendid ; in the spring things will pick up with God's help. Rent a meadow from the barynia and you 'll have your hay. Take a load or two into town, and you 'll have money in your pockets ; then you can sell some of the winter corn. Take some rye into market—there 's money again ; and then oats too there are for sale. And next year you will soon see how instead of these little huts that the fire ate up there will be beautiful new houses, large and comfortable, and you will all live in them, each under his own roof, in gladness and happiness, and will thank the Lord for the blessing He sent you. You will see.'

And Aunt Tatiana kept walking helplessly about the ruins of her house, turning over the smouldering timber, and calling :

' Pete, Pete ! Where are you, my lovey ? Answer me ' ; and did not hear how Kalistratitch, an old, old man, was saying to her :

' Maybe he 's run off to the woods. I saw him. I was sitting on the barn steps when your house took fire. And there he was running round and round in the room, his little shirt flapping. I cried out to him, " Push the door open, dearie, push the door ! " But he kept running round and round, and then I couldn't see any more. I expect he has run off to the woods from fright.'

But Tatiana could feel nothing except that her heart was breaking to pieces.

' Pete, Pete ! Where are you, my lovey ? Answer me ! ' her cry sounded above the general talk.

At last one or two people took pity on her and came to her help. They turned up the fallen roof and under its smoking ruins found the little boy's body. The uppermost half of the corpse was a formless, charred black mass ; the side turned towards the floor was untouched.

Tatiana fell back, everything went black before her eyes, and from her throat came a cry that rang through the whole village :

' Oh God ! Do you see ? '

The priest also heard the cry, and of course hastened to her with consolatory words.

' Why this plaint ? ' he said to her with kindly re-proach. ' And do you remember Job ? No ? Then I will remind you. He was rich and famous, he had chil-dren, and cattle, and treasure, and suddenly, by the will of God, everything was taken from him : children, and cattle, and friends ; and he himself was stricken with leprosy, driven out from the town, and lay at the gates upon ashes. Dogs licked his sores—dogs ! But in spite of all this he not only did not complain, but still more loved the Lord who had created him. And the Lord, seeing his faithfulness, looked kindly upon him. After a time he was restored to health and riches, and became more famous than before. His flocks increased, enough children were born unto him, indeed everything . . .'

But the priest's words of comfort reached Tatiana only as so much confused and annoying noise. She gazed with a fixed stare on the line which divided the untouched from the charred half on Petushka's body and kept whispering softly, ' Oh God, do You see ? '

In the manor-house that day the kind barynia, Anna Andreyevna Koréyshchikova was celebrating her birthday. There were not many guests, but all were her sincere friends—the Leader of the Nobility, Kipyashchev and his wife, the Captain of the Police and his niece, and also Ivan Ivanitch Glaz, a civilian. People said that in his presence one should keep one's mouth shut. However, as the whole company consisted of people in whose company one had better not let one's tongue wag (Anna Andreyevna herself used to say that she was on ' government service ' somewhere), Ivan Ivanitch felt quite at home among them. The priest and his wife were present also.

Anna Andreyevna was a general's widow, some forty odd years old, still handsome and specially remarkable at balls and evening parties, where décolleté was obligatory, and where her bust drew the gaze of men of all ages and of all weapons. But she had once for all said to herself, ' Ni, ni, c'est fini,' and gave her life wholly to her children. This caused society to say of her, ' C'est une sainte,' and for her patriotism she was styled ' fière matrone.' Like all Russian ladies, she spoke French, knew un peu d'Arithmétique, un peu de Géographie, et un peu de Mythologie (cette pauvre Léda !), had lived much abroad, and had lately become a patriot and taken to loving ' the good Russian people.' Three years ago she had visited her birthplace, Gorbilevo, and since then spent every summer there. She built a mausoleum to her late husband in the garden, and said her prayers every day. She made no acquaintances except among ' the tried friends of order,' did not concern herself with agriculture, but rented her land to the peasants, and evidently economised. She had a son, Seregya, a law student of sixteen, and an eighteen-year-old daughter, Vérochka, an acute little person, who also knew *un peu d'Arithmétique et un peu de Mythologie.*

The gentry had already come back from church and were at dinner when some one ran in to say that Sophoníha was on fire. The priest immediately disappeared to administer comfort ; the rest ran to the windows to look. Behind the enormous cloud of smoke the flames were not visible, but the smoke was blown straight in the direction of the manor-house and they were aware of its acrid smell. There were no villagers to be seen, either, but along the road ran crowds of neighbouring peasants and people from the manor.

' Say what you like, friends,' said Anna Andreyevna at last, ' I cannot remain a passive spectator. They are mine. Wicked people have parted us [1]—I hope only temporarily—but I still remember that they are— mine.'

But she was not allowed to carry out this self-sacrificing act alone, and the whole assembly offered to accompany her.

' Of course, anyhow it 's our duty,' continued Anna

[1] *I.e.* by freeing the serfs.—*Tr.*

Andreyevna. 'Even if they were not my peasants it would still be our duty to be on the scene of suffering. We have been impoverished, we have been bullied—but we have forgotten it all. We remember only that to us is turned the gaze of a suffering younger brother.'

Learning that that day bread had been baked for the servants and the manor-workpeople, she ordered several loaves to be cut into slices and taken to the peasants who had suffered from the fire.

'We can bake again to-morrow for our own people,' she said. 'We must do something for these. And don't forget to sprinkle it with salt.'

In a word, she did everything she possibly could, and finally caught up her purse, saying, 'That's for emergencies!' And Vérochka, following her mother's example, took her purse with her own little bright silver pieces.

The company stopped just outside the village, but Vérochka and Mlle Shipyashchaya[1] impulsively went on along the street.

'Tell the peasants I give them a present of two quarters of rye,' Anna Andreyevna called after them.

In five minutes or so, Vérochka came running back in tears.

'Oh, mother darling!' she announced, 'there's a poor woman there whose little boy has been burnt. Oh, how terrible! She is in such a state! Bátiushka[2]

---

[1] From 'hiss.'—*Tr.*
[2] Little father; *i.e.* the priest.—*Tr.*

is trying to comfort her, but she takes no notice and only keeps repeating " Oh God, do You see ? " Mother darling, it 's terrible, terrible, terrible ! '

' It 's dreadful for her ; but how worked up you are, Vera ! ' Anna Andreyevna said reproachfully. ' That will never do, my love. There 's a Purpose in all things —we must always remember ! Of course . . . it 's a great loss ; but there are worse losses still, and we bow our heads and bear them. Do you remember Baymakov's bankruptcy and our current account ? . . . He paid six per cent.—and then ! However, a nightingale is not fed on fables, as the saying goes. Friends,' she added, turning to her companions, ' let us make a little collection for the poor bereaved mother ! Just what each feels he can spare.'

With a trembling hand she took a ten-rouble note from her purse, and put it on her outstretched palm. Vérochka immediately added her whole purse ; the guests also contributed some small notes. Only Ivan Ivanitch Glaz looked the other way, whistling. About thirty roubles were collected.

' There—take these to her,' said Anna Andrey-evna. ' Tell her there are kind people in the world still. And tell the peasants again about the rye—two quarters. Have they brought the bread ? Tell them to hand it round. That 's to stay the first pangs of hunger.'

Vérochka ran along quickly. At that moment she fancied herself a guardian angel, sailing on silver wings in the blue sky with thirty roubles in her hands. She found Tatiana still in the same position. The woman was standing with wide-open eyes, mechanically moving her lips without the least sign of being aware of anything. Bátiushka was standing beside her as before, relating to her incidents in the lives of the early martyrs under the wicked Emperor Nero. Tatiana had not yet thought of what was to become of her—whether she would need a house, fields, and all the other things that had hitherto filled her life, or whether she would have to roam the world working for hire.

And suddenly—here was the guardian angel !

'Here, dear, mamma has sent you this !' said Vérochka, holding the money out to her.

Tatiana understood nothing—did not even glance at the alms.

'Take it, you stubborn woman,' the Bátiushka admonished her. 'The kind lady has sent you this, and you scorn it.'

The peasants who stood round took an interest in it too, and began to admonish her.

'Take it, Aunt Tatiana, take it, if it 's given to you. It 'll help towards your house . . . take it !'

Tatiana did not stir.

Vérochka stood a little while, then put the money on to the ground, and went off hurt. Bátiushka picked it up. 'Well, if you don't want it, I 'll use it for Church decoration,' he said. 'The lustre is rather poor, so we 'll sell that for lumber, and along with what is here we 'll get a new one ! Be witnesses, believers !'

' Mother darling, she wouldn't take it ! ' Vérochka said with tears in her voice.

They were all astonished.

' So there 's that sort of spirit in them still ! It 's not been thrashed out of them yet,' enunciated Mr. Glaz cryptically.

But this time Anna Andreyevna did not agree with him.

' There is that spirit, it 's true, but we should not lose sight of the profound nature of her grief ! Only a mother's heart can understand what it is to lose a son ! '

The priest's prophecy was fulfilled. Some two years later I was driving past Sophonīha and saw a veritable metamorphosis. In place of the charred ruins there were orderly rows of new houses, high, and fairly roomy. The roofs, it is true, were thatched with straw, but well clipped, so that there were no wisps or untidy ends to offend the eye. The new timber shone in the sun like shelled eggs. Only on Tatiana's plot there were still charred bits of wood lying about. She herself had disappeared from the village—no one knew where. Probably she was journeying among holy places, a pilgrim begging her bread. The peasants lived together in peace, and therefore lived well. They worked hard, paid their serf-money [1] and their taxes, and tendered their services to the government, sent recruits, horse-transport, and post-horses. And even if something over

---

[1] *I.e.* the money for the land allotted to them when they were freed from serfdom.—*Tr.*

and above was required of them they gave it readily. Shipyashchy, the Captain of the Police, cannot praise them enough.

'That village is A1 on my books!' he says.

Good luck to you, my lads!

THE SELF-SACRIFICING
RABBIT

Once the rabbit got into trouble with the wolf. He was running past the wolf's lair, you see, and the wolf saw him and cried out, ' Stop a minute, bunny dear ! ' But the rabbit not only did not stop, but just ran the faster. So the wolf caught him up in three bounds, and said, ' In punishment for not stopping at my first word, this is my judgment : I condemn you to loss of life by being torn up. And as I am not hungry just now, and my mate is not hungry, and we have a supply for some five days yet, you just sit under a bush and wait your turn. And perhaps . . . ha, ha . . . I will pardon you ! '

The rabbit sat on his haunches under a bush without moving. He only thought of one thing : in how many days and in what manner death must come. He would glance to the side, where the wolf's lair was, and the wolf's eye would be looking at him. And sometimes it was worse still—the wolf and his mate would come out and walk up and down the green in front of him. They would look at him and the wolf would say something to his mate in wolf-language and both would burst out, ' ha, ha, ha.' And the wolf cubs coming along, too, would trot up to him, playfully gnashing their teeth . . . while his heart would sink into his paws !

Never had he loved life as he did then. He was a well-conducted rabbit, he had looked out the daughter of a rabbit widow and wanted to get married. It was to her, to his intended, that he was running when the wolf collared him. His intended may have thought, ' He is faithless to me, my Lopears ! ' And perhaps she waited a bit, and then . . . loved some one else. And perhaps it was like this : she was playing in the bushes, poor darling, and the wolf . . . nabbed and ate her up. . . .

The poor fellow, thinking all this, sat bathed in tears. There they go, the rabbit dreams ! He thought to get married, to buy a samovar, dreamt of drinking tea with his young rabbit wife, and instead—this ! And how many hours were there left till death ?

There he sat one night, dozing. He dreamt that the wolf had made him chief official secretary, and while the rabbit was away, *he* went paying calls on his rabbit wife. . . . Suddenly he felt some one nudging him. He looked round—and it was his intended's brother.

' Your intended is dying,' he said. ' She heard what a misfortune had befallen you, and straightway sickened. Now all she thinks of is, " Shall I have to die and not even say good-bye to my dear ? " '

The condemned rabbit heard these words and his heart was rent in pieces. What was it for ? Why had he deserved his dreadful fate ? He had lived openly, done no revolutionising, not gone out armed, was bound on his own business. Did he deserve death for this ? Death ? Think what a word ! And death not only for him alone, but for her too, his little grey bunny, whose only fault was that she had loved him with all her heart. Oh, how he longed to fly to her, to take her, the little grey one, by the ears with his paws, and pet her and stroke her little head !

' Let us fly ! ' the emissary said meanwhile.

Hearing these words, the condemned prisoner was transfigured for a moment. He gathered himself up into a bunch and laid his ears back. Another moment and he would have been off. He should not have looked at the wolf's lair at that moment, but he did look. And the rabbit heart sank.

' I can't,' he says, ' till the wolf gives me permission.'

And the wolf, meanwhile, seeing and hearing everything, whispered with his wife, evidently commending the rabbit for his high-mindedness.

' Let us fly ! ' said the messenger again.

' I can't,' repeated the prisoner.

' What are you whispering there, plotting together ? ' the wolf bawled suddenly.

The rabbits just went faint, both of them. The messenger was caught too. Instigation of a sentinel to flight—what is the punishment for that, pray ? Ah, the little grey bunny would have to go without her betrothed and her brother too—the wolf would gobble them both up !

The rabbits came to, and there, before them, the wolf and his wife stood, and their eyes shone like lamps in the darkness.

' We 're . . . we 're not doing anything, your Excellency . . . just talking . . . my relative just came to see me . . .' the condemned rabbit mumbled, simply fainting with fright meanwhile.

133

' " Just talking." . . . I know you ! Don't trust you far. What is it then ? '

' It 's like this, your Excellency,' the bride's brother put in, ' my sister, who is engaged to him, is dying, so she has sent me to ask if he can't be allowed to go and say good-bye to her.'

' Hm ! It 's good that the bride loves her betrothed. That means they will have a lot of little ones—there will be more for the wolves to eat. We love each other, the wolf and I, and we have lots of little ones. Ever so many out in the world already, and four are living with us yet. Wolf, should we not let the rabbit go and say good-bye to her ? '

' But we meant to eat him the day after to-morrow...'

' I 'll come back, your Excellency. I 'll put it through that quick. . . . On my honour, I will,' the prisoner hastened to add, and so that there should be no doubt that he *could* put it through, he cocked his ears and looked such a dare-devil fellow, that even the wolf was struck with admiration and thought, ' Ah, if only I had soldiers like that ! '

And the she-wolf grew pensive and said :

' There now—nothing but a rabbit, and see how he loves his mate ! '

Well, there was nothing for it—the wolf consented to give leave to the rabbit, but on condition that he should put it through exactly to time. And the bride's brother to be kept as hostage.

' If you 're not back in two days at six o'clock in the morning,' he said, ' I will eat him instead of you ; and

134

if you return—I will eat you both—or perhaps . . . ha, ha . . . I may pardon you ! '

Lopears was off like an arrow. The earth shook as he ran. If a mountain was in the way, he would scale it full pelt ; a river, and he did not even look out for a ford, but slap across it, swimming ; a bog—he leapt from the fifth tuft to the tenth. It was no joke to get to this far-off kingdom, to go to the baths, to get married (' I shall certainly get married,' he kept saying to himself), and then get back in time for the wolf's breakfast.

Even the birds were astounded at his speed. They said, ' In the *Moscovskye Viedomosti* they say that a rabbit has no soul—only vapour—and just see what a lick he goes ! '

Well, he got back at last. What rejoicing there was, tongue cannot tell nor pen write. The little grey bunny no sooner saw her beloved than she forgot all her ills. She stood on her hind legs, took a drum, and began to drum out the cavalry trot with her paws. This was a surprise she had prepared for her dear.

And the rabbit widow nearly went off her head. She did not know how to make enough of her future son-in-law, what to give him to eat of the best, where to put him to sit.

And aunts and cousins and sisters came running in from everywhere. They all wanted to have a look at the bridegroom, and maybe pick up a meal or two.

But the bridegroom did not seem himself at all. He

had scarcely exchanged loving greetings with his fiancée when he began saying : ' I 'd better have a bath and get married right away.'

' What 's the hurry ? ' asked the rabbit mother chaffingly.

' Got to get back. Only one day's leave.' And he told them how it all was. He told them, and the tears kept running down his face. He did not want to go back, and yet how could he not go back, for he had given his word and a rabbit is true to his word.

All the aunts and cousins sat in council. They unanimously came to the conclusion, ' You have spoken the truth, Lopears. Before giving your word, hold out, but having given it, keep to it. Never in all rabbit history has it happened that rabbits cheated.'

A tale is soon told, but affairs among rabbits are still sooner done. Towards the morning the knot was tied, towards the evening he was already saying farewell to his young wife.

' The wolf will eat me for sure,' he said, ' then be faithful to me. If you have children, bring them up strictly. Best of all, send them into the circus. There they will teach them not only to beat the drum, but even to shoot peas out of a cannon ! '

And suddenly, as in a dream—he must have remembered the wolf again—he added : ' And perhaps . . . ha, ha . . . he may pardon me.'

That 's all they saw of him !

In the meantime, while Lopears was enjoying himself and putting his wedding through, in the country which lay between his home and the wolf's lair great disasters had happened.

In one place there had been heavy rains, so that the river which the day before the rabbit had swum quite easily, had swollen over a good ten miles. In another place King Aaron had declared war upon King Nikita, and a battle raged right in the rabbit's path. In a third place cholera had broken out, and the rabbit had to go a hundred miles round to miss quarantine. And besides, wolves, foxes, owls, watched him at every step. He was a clever Lopears. He had reckoned so as to have three hours to the good, but when, one after another, these difficulties arose, his heart grew cold within him. He ran all evening, he ran half the night. His feet were cut about with stones, on his sides the fur hung in lumps, torn by prickly branches. His mouth foamed with blood, his eyes were well-nigh sightless, and he with all this way still to go, and all the time his friend the hostage stood before him as in the flesh. He was standing sentinel before the wolf's lair, thinking, ' In so many hours my dear brother-in-law will be coming to relieve me.'

He would think of this and put on speed. Mountains, nor forests, nor bogs, nothing daunted him. How often his heart was fit to break, but he mastered his heart too, so that his fruitless agitation should not keep him from his purpose. This was not the time for grief nor tears. Let all emotion be still, if only he could rescue his friend from the wolf's jaws.

And now day was breaking. Owls, bats, all night-beasts trailed off to sleep. The air felt cold. And suddenly all around was still, as if in death, and Lopears still ran on, and still but with one thought : ' Is it possible I shall not be in time to rescue him ? ' The East reddened—but on the distant horizon flame seemed to spurt upon the clouds, then more and still more. Then all at once the dew upon the grass burned with fire, the day-birds awoke, the ants crawled out, the worms, the beetles ; smoke drifted up from somewhere. Through the rye a whisper ran louder and louder, but Lopears saw nothing, and only kept repeating, ' I have done for my friend, I have done for him ! ' At last here was the mountain, beyond this a bog, and in it the wolf's lair. He was late, the Lopears, he was late !

He gathered his remaining strength. He leaped on to the mountain top—reached it—but he could no longer run. He fell exhausted. . . . Was it possible that he would not reach the place ?

He saw the wolf's lair before him as in a saucer. Somewhere in the distance a church clock struck six, and each stroke fell like a hammer-blow upon the poor beast. At the last stroke the wolf rose from his lair, stretched himself, and wagged his tail with pleasure. He walked up to the hostage, flattened him down with his paw, dug his claws into his belly to tear him in half for himself and his mate. The little ones, running up, sat round, champing their teeth, learning.

' Here I am, here ! ' shouted Lopears, like a hundred thousand rabbits all together, and rolled down the mountain side into the bog. And the wolf commended him.

' I see,' he said, ' that one can trust a rabbit. And this is my judgment : sit here till further notice under this bush and some day I will . . . ha, ha . . . pardon you ! '

THE UNSLEEPING EYE

In a certain country, in a certain kingdom, once upon a time, there lived a Public Prosecutor, and he had two eyes : one—a sleeping eye, and the other an unsleeping eye. With the sleeping eye he saw nothing at all, and with the unsleeping eye he saw things that did not matter.

In that kingdom, of old there had been a custom : as soon as an inhabitant had a little son with two eyes—a sleeping one, and an unsleeping one—in the Census Returns was put down : ' The inhabitant Dodger Tricksterov, in the Marshes,[1] has had a little boy named Public Prosecutor.' And then they waited till the boy came of age.

And so it was in this case. Scarcely had the laddie grown higher than the ground than they sent along to him : ' Pray step up.'

' With pleasure. But how soon will there be a vacancy in the Senate ? '

' Oh, certainly. Directly. At once.'

' Aha ! '

The little lad squared his chest and looked in the glass. Who was that shy creature peeping out at him ? Why, it was he himself ! All right. And without so much as a naughty word, he set to work directly ; with his sleeping eye seeing nothing, and with his unsleeping eye seeing things that did not matter. ' I am here,' he

---

[1] A district in Moscow.—*Tr.*

says, ' just for a minute, on my way to the Senate, and there I shall close both eyes. And my ears too by that time will be stopped up, with God's help.'

The extortioners, the slanderers, the murderers, the robbers, and the thieves saw the laddie looking at them with his unsleeping eye and took fright instantly. They thought and thought what to do about it, and all decided to leave the unsleeping side and take shelter beneath the Public Prosecutor's sleeping eye. And on the un-sleeping side it became as clean and clear as if there never had been any evil-doers or thieves or murderers, but only ordinary liars, cheats, traitors, turncoats, and bigots, whom the Public Prosecutor, properly speaking, had no business with. And the laddie saw how from one glance of his unsleeping eye an unclouded prospect opened up, and rejoiced. Surely, he thought, the Authorities would note his zealous efforts !

And he strutted up and down the field of administra-tive justice like a cock of the walk. He went strutting and shouting, ' Look out, look out ! I 'll drown you in a teaspoon ! '

Suddenly he saw a man standing, calling out loudly : ' Help ! I am robbed. Help ! ' Of course he ran up to the robbed man.

' What are you yelling the place down for ? I 'll give you something to shout about ! you good-for-nothing ! '

' Why, Mr. Public Prosecutor—thieves ! '

' Where ? What thieves ? You lie : there are no thieves, and never have been any ' (and they meanwhile hiding under his nostril, on the sleeping side). ' You miscreant, you trouble the Authorities with complaints unworthy of attention ! . . . Arrest him ! '

He went on, and heard : ' Extortioners, Mr. Public Prosecutor, extortioners have ruined me ! Usurers, evil-doers, adulterers ! '

' Where ? What extortioners ? I don't see any extortioners ! You make this row on purpose, you dogs, to undermine authority. Arrest him ! '

He went on farther, and heard : ' They are stealing private and public property ! What are you about, Mr. Public Prosecutor ? There they are, the vultures —there they are ! '

' Where ? Who is stealing public property ? '

' There they are—there ! Look what a great house this man has put up on stolen money ! And this one— look ! See how many dessiatins of State land he has pinched ! '

' You lie, you good-for-nothings ! They are not thieves—they are the owners of property. They quietly hold their property and all their documents are in order. It 's you evil idlers shout and yell in order to undermine the principle of ownership ! Arrest him ! '

The farther he went, the worse it got.

' Here 's a wife nagging her husband to death from morning till night.'

' Here 's a husband driving his wife into her coffin.'
' You don't look after anything, Mr. Public Prosecutor.'

' I look after nothing ? And have you seen what an eye I have ? One, it is true, but ah ! what a way I can see with it ! So far, that I can even see your rubbishy

soul through and through ! And I know what riff-raff
like you are trying to get at ! You want to undermine
the institution of the family ! Arrest him ! '

He went through all the institutions and found everywhere that of themselves they stood firm and indestructible, but the chatterers would do for them altogether if
one did not shut their mouths in time. And when the
laddie came to the Institution of Government he did not
even stop to talk. He just yelled out, as if on a sudden
illumined, ' Seize him ! Bind him ! Shut him in ! Wall
him up ! ' And while he shouted, the unsleeping eye
went spinning round in his head like a catherine wheel.

The whole day long the laddie slaved like this, safe-
guarding the institutions, and towards the evening he
would come back and rest. He would lie on the bed
and think : ' Everything I have carried out fully, as
the Authorities desire ! Extortioners, venial officials,
wicked men and malpractisers I have scattered with the
help of my unsleeping eye above, and as for those who
undermine institutions, and who trouble the Authorities
with vain complaints, I have dealt with them extra
specially. And all is clean and pleasing to view. I
hope that the Authorities on their side will value my
services accordingly in due measure.'

' What could I wish for you ? ' he used to say to himself. ' To the Senate ? But then I can still hear with
one ear. Besides, the Senate will not run away. . .
Perhaps . . . perhaps into the . . . But no, that 'll be for
when I 've lost the sense of smell too ! No, but now,
in the immediate future, what could I wish for ? '

143

He egged on his imagination and tickled it up, till at last it was quite out of sorts. ' I must get married as soon as possible ; that 's what I must do.'

And as he brought the unsleeping eye into action for finding the bride, of course he soon found one. . . . Namely, Miss Agrippina, a young lady of such beauty as tongue cannot tell nor pen write of. And with her, twenty thousand—just exactly as with a ticket for the Government Loan Lottery.

He got married. They gave a splendid wedding feast in Zavitaev's restaurant, and then went to their new home together. But suddenly the laddie looked, and for some reason the newly-married bride was hiding in the shelter of the sleeping eye.

He looked here, he looked there.

' Agrippina, where are you ? '

' I am not Agrippina, I am Agatha. And my Saint's name-day is on the 5th of February.'

Here was a go ! The laddie even went pale with fright. Could the devil have taken a hand in his career ?

' Come out—Agatha ! ' he cried.

He looked—and Agatha, like himself, had one sleeping and one unsleeping eye. Only his unsleeping eye was on the left side and hers on the right. It seemed as if Fate itself had intended them to run the business of Public Prosecutor together.

' Have you got a dowry ? '

' I 've no dowry either, only one unsleeping eye. That 's all.'

Oh, the devil take it ! She was Agrippina all the

time and then all of a sudden went and turned into
Agatha! He set to work investigating how such a
thing could have occurred—and it appeared that it was
very simple. While he turned his unsleeping eye
steadily in one direction, Agrippina ran out for a minute
and got married to an officer. And he took—Agatha!

Well, there was nothing to be done about it. The
money for the wedding feast was already paid out to
Zavitaev—they had to live somehow. They lay down
to sleep. But as they lay there looking at each other
with their unsleeping eyes it gave him the creeps. But
she did not turn a hair—rather liked it even.

' Are you an old witch ? ' he asked her. ' Tell me.'

' No, I am not an old witch, but your lawful wedded
wife. And up till now I have been doing a trade in
stolen socks at the Aprassin market.'

' How stolen ? How is it I did not catch you ? '

' You can't catch any one. You keep staring one
way with your unsleeping eye, and never see what is
happening under your left nostril.'

' Well, let's catch thieves together, if that's so—I
on the right and you on the left.'

In short, so well did they fix things up that in a
year's time they had a little son, and he too had an
unsleeping eye.

' What a queer fish ! ' exclaimed the laddie when he
saw his first-born.

It was only then that he jumped to it that, however
valuable one unsleeping eye is, two ordinary ones are
perhaps of more value still.

His official duties in the meantime went on being fulfilled in due course. Gradually he filled all the prisons with fussers, while extortioners, concessionaires, and other evil-doers prospered in the shelter of his sleeping eye.

Well, after a time he began to get hard of hearing in both ears, and even the unsleeping eye began to close gradually. It was the very time, then, to hurry up into the Senate, while he had not yet lost his sense of smell.

Then he heard them calling him !

He put on a flannel vest, warm socks, pulled on a pair of felt boots, stopped up his ears a little with hemp, scented himself with camphor oil, wrapped himself up in a fur coat, and over that Agatha tied a woolly scarf, and he went to the Senate. He walked along thinking, ' I wonder what I 'll dream in my first sleep in the Senate ? '

But here something unexpected occurred. While he kept directing his unsleeping eye steadily to the right, the Senate went and turned a bit to the left, just under the sleeping eye. The Public Prosecutor searched and searched—he sniffed with his nose and clicked his tongue and even felt all round with his hands—but for the life of him he could not lay his hand on the Senate.

At last he saw a policeman awake at his post, so naturally he made straight for him. Told him all about it. ' Now, my man, can you tell me where the Senate has got to ? '

The policeman looked at him and instantly read his unsleeping soul.

146

'I can,' he said; 'here's the Senate. There it is, gleaming in the sun! watching to see that no mischievous creature trades on the law.... Just look at you now! But, you see, it's not for every one we've kept a place in the Senate. You, now, kept gazing with your unsleeping eye, and couldn't see an inch beyond your nose, and we've orders not to admit folks like that these days. You'd better go back home, old gentleman, take off your felt boots, rub your eyes, syringe your ears, and go and lie down to sleep on top of the stove alongside of your old woman. For our regulations here now are: folks' heads and legs and other members all in their proper place, and every one's eyes and ears—wide open!'

And so that Public Prosecutor never got to the Senate at all.

THE RAM WHO COULD NOT
REMEMBER

'Sheep have been enslaved by man from
prehistoric times : their real ancestors
are unknown.'   *Brehm.*

Whether the tame sheep has ever been wild, history
does not relate. In the very earliest times patriarchs
already had flocks of tame sheep, and thereafter
throughout the ages the sheep appears over the whole
face of the earth as an animal specially created for the
use of man. Man, in his turn, produces entirely new
species of sheep, having very little in common with each
other. Some are reared for meat, some for fat, some
for their skins, some for their warm soft fleece.

The tame sheep themselves least of all, of course,
remember their free ancestors, but simply consider
themselves as belonging to the species in which the
moment of their birth finds them. This moment forms
the point of departure of the sheep's personal history,
but even this gradually vanishes as the sheep approaches
maturity. So that a truly wise sheep remembers
nothing except the grass, hay, and chaff given it to eat.

However, sin and misfortune wait on no man, as the
saying goes. A certain ram sleeping, once saw a dream.
Evidently he saw something besides fodder in his dream,
for he awoke troubled, and looked about him a long
time as if seeking something with his eyes.

He tried to remember what it was that had happened but could recall only a distance, veiled in silvery light, and nothing more. Nothing but the vague feeling of this formless silvery space was left, but no definite outline, not one actual shape. . . .

'Sheep! I say, sheep! what did I dream?' he asked the sheep who lay beside him, and who, being a veritable sheep, had never in her life dreamt dreams.

'Go to sleep, story-teller!' the sheep said crossly. 'You weren't brought from across the sea to have dreams and to show off like that.'

The ram was a pedigree English Merino. The squire, Ivan Sosontitch Rastakovsky, had paid unheard-of sums for him and had great hopes of him. But of course he had not brought him from across the sea to have a generation of *clever* sheep from him, but a breed with a very fine fleece.

And at first, on arrival, the ram bid fair to make a very good reputation for himself. He thought about nothing, took an interest in nothing, he did not even understand where and why he was brought—he just quite simply existed. As for the question, what precisely is the ram or sheep, and what are their rights and duties, on these subjects the ram not only conducted no propaganda, but did not even suspect that such questions could disturb sheep's heads. And this attitude helped him to fulfil a sheep's duties so scrupulously and conscientiously that Ivan Sosontitch could not think enough of him, and used to bring his neighbours to look—'there!'

And then suddenly this dream. . . . What sort of dream it was the ram could not for the life of him remember. He only felt that into his existence there had come something unusual, something disturbing—a sadness and a longing.

His shed seemingly was just the same, the fodder the same, and the same was the herd of sheep given him to perfect, and yet it seemed as if he could take no heed of it. He wandered about the shed with a lost air, and only blayed : ' What did I see in my dreams ? Tell me what I saw.'

But the sheep did not evince the least sympathy for him in his agitation, and even called him with not a little spitefulness ' clever creature,' and ' philosopher,' which words, as is well known, in sheep's language have an even worse meaning than ' bad form.'

From the time when he began dreaming dreams, they remembered with regret the plain ram of simple blood who had bullied them for seven years previously, but in the end for his services was told off to the kitchen and there disappeared without trace (he was only seen being borne in triumph on a dish from the kitchen to the master's house). Now that was a proper, useful ram. He never dreamt any dreams, never had any disquieting feelings, but just did his duty punctually by the dictates of the sheep's code of rules—and troubled about nothing else. And what happened? This old and trusted servant was dismissed, and in his place they put an idle, dreaming creature, who from morning till night blayed goodness knows about what, and meanwhile the sheep went sterile.

' Not much perfecting that English fool will do for us,' the sheep complained to Nikìta the shepherd. ' I hope we shan't get into a row with Ivan Sosontitch all through him.'

' Don't you worry, my dears,' Nikìta said to them encouragingly, ' we 'll shear him to-morrow, then whip him with nettles a bit, and he 'll be as good as gold.'

But Nikìta's hopes were not fulfilled. The ram was shorn, whipped—and that very night he saw a dream again.

From this time the dreams never left him. No sooner did he double his legs up under him than slumber over-took him—day or night—in the yard.

And no sooner did he shut his eyes than he seemed wholly transformed, and his face would become not sheeplike, but serious, austere, like an old wise peasant man's, the sort they used to nickname ' ministers ' in old days. So that any one passing would certainly have said, ' A farmyard is no place for this ram—he should be a burgomaster.'

Nevertheless, however much he was on the qui vive to reconstruct the dream he had just seen, his efforts were always unavailing.

He remembered in his dream that vivid figures passed before him, and even whole scenes, the contemplation of which brought him ecstasy—but as soon as he awoke, the figures and the scenes disappeared he did not know whither, and he again became an ordinary ram. The only difference was, that whereas formerly he went boldly forward to meet a ram's duties, now he wandered

151

about as if stunned and seeking something everywhere
—but what precisely—he could not explain to himself.
A ram—and a melancholiac at that—what could he
expect in the future except the knife ?

But even besides the prospect of the knife, the ram's
position was in itself deeply painful.

There is no pain more bitter than that which is
brought by the impotent striving from darkness to light
of a disturbed unconsciousness. Overcome by the
sudden longing of formless hopes, the poor overwhelmed
creature flung himself to and fro, growing weak and
faint, but unable to know the nature of these hopes, nor
yet their source. He felt his heart aflame, and did not
know for what this flame was lit ; he dimly felt that the
world did not end at the walls of his pen, that beyond
those walls stretched brilliant, rainbow-coloured dis-
tances ; he dimly felt space, light, freedom—yet could
not tell what light and space and freedom were. . . . As
the ram's dreams became more frequent, his agitation
grew. Nowhere did he meet sympathy or understanding. The sheep huddled closer together at his approach ; the shepherd, Nikìta, although he evidently
knew something about it, was stubbornly silent. He
was a wise old peasant who knew all there was to know
about sheep-keeping, and recognised only one rule :

' If you are born in the sheep's walk of life,' he used
to say solemnly, ' stay there.'

But this was just what the ram was unable to do.
It was precisely the ' walk of life ' that tormented him,
not because his life was hard, but because ever since he

began to have dreams, he was constantly aware of some quite different ' walk of life.'

He could not reconstruct these dreams, but his instincts were so strongly roused, that in spite of the inexplicable nature of his inner perturbation, he could no longer cope with it.

Nevertheless in the course of time this perturbation began to die down, and he seemed even to have become more staid.   But this was not in consequence of a sober resolution to tread in the sheep's regular course, but rather of a general exhaustion of the ram's organism. So there was no good to be got out of him.

He slept—evidently of set purpose—from morning till night, as if he tried to find in dreaming those sensations of happiness which he could not re-establish in his waking state. . . .

Meanwhile daily he pined and sickened, and at length grew so emaciated that the silly sheep on seeing him would begin to sneeze and whisper together mockingly. And as the strange malady gained on him, his face became more and more intelligent.   The shepherds all pitied him.   They all knew that he was an honest and good-hearted ram, and that if he had not fulfilled the master's hopes it was through no fault of his, but because of some deep misfortune which had befallen him —a misfortune not usual among sheep, but—as many guessed instinctively—doing him personally great honour.

Ivan Sosontitch himself was very sympathetic to the ram's sufferings.   More than once the shepherd

Nikìta hinted that the best solution in this queer business was the knife, but Rastakovsky firmly refused.

' He has made a hole in my purse,' he said, ' but not in order just to use his skin. Let him die his own death.'

At last the longed-for moment of illumination came. Above the fields a June night bathed in moonlight hung glimmering ; all round was impenetrable silence ; not only men were hushed, but all Nature seemed to lie motionless, as if under a magic spell.

All slept in the fold. The sheep, with drooping heads, dozed by the fence. The ram lay solitary in the middle of the fold. Suddenly he leapt up as in alarm. He straightened his legs, stretched out his neck, lifted his head, and then a tremor ran through his whole body. In this position of expectancy, as if he listened, his gaze intently fixed on something, he stood a few moments, and then a loud heart-breaking cry burst from his throat.

Hearing this agonising sound, the sheep jumped from their places and flung themselves to the side. The sheep-dog, waking too, ran barking to restore order in the terrified herd. But the ram no longer heeded the disturbance : his whole being was engrossed in contemplation. Before his fading gaze was unfolding the secret of his dream.

One more moment—and his body trembled for the last time. Then his legs doubled up under him and he crashed dead to the ground.

Ivan Sosontitch was grieved by his death.

' What can be the reason of it ? ' he mused aloud. ' He was a ram like any other and then suddenly . . .

Nikìta ! you have been a shepherd these fifty years, you must know their fool ways ; tell me why should we have had this misfortune ? '

' Must have seen the free ram in a dream,' Nikìta answered ; ' saw him, you know, but couldn't take it in as it might be. . . . So he took on about it and then died. It 's just as among us now . . .'

But Ivan Sosontitch cut short further explanations.

' Let this be a lesson to us,' he said approvingly to Nikìta. ' Somewhere else this ram might have turned into a goat—but in our parts the rule is : if you are a ram, stay a ram without any nonsense. Your master will be well off and you will be well off, and the State is pleased. And you 'll have plenty of everything : grass and hay and chaff. And the sheep will be nice to you. . . . Isn't that so, Nikìta ? '

' That 's just so, Ivan Sosontitch,' answered Nikìta.

THE SISKIN'S TRAGEDY

The Canary was given in marriage to the Siskin and the wedding was splendid. At the shop called ' Work and Play ' they bought a new little wooden church ; the pastor was a learned Bullfinch ; Starlings sang the bridal songs, and to keep order the police master sent a company of Sparrow Hawks. Nearly all the birds of the forest came to have a look at the young pair, and there were not a few honoured guests too. Best man to the Siskin was the Chaffinch, and to the Canary, the Nightingale. The Vulture himself hinted that he would like to give the bride away, but the parents found a polite excuse to decline that honour, and invited the deaf Heath-Cock—the one who as long ago as the time of King Peascod was put into the Senate in consideration of his senility and loss of memory.

The young pair, the parents, and the guests—all made merry. The Siskin carried himself bravely, tasting beforehand the sweets of married bliss. The Canary preened her feathers ; the parents thought, ' Well, thank goodness we 've got one daughter off ! ' and the guests looked forward to the heap of hempseed, pickled gnats, sugared flies, etc., which they were about to demolish at the Siskin's house-warming. Only the ill-omened Crow cawed for no reason : ' No good will come of this marriage—no good, no good ! '

Although among men the Crow is accounted stupid, all birds know that if she caws, she has good reason so to do. And indeed, scarcely had her voice sounded, than the Cuckoo called out : ' Cuckoo ! What if it should come to pass as the bird of ill omen predicts ? ' And after her the Blue Tit, the Redtail, and the Peewit whistled words to the same effect.

And every one set to work observing the young pair, and remembering. They turned to the intimate history of these two beings, tied a moment ago with an irrevocable knot, remembered their inclinations, their tastes, their habits. And as usual, the result was a picture.

The Siskin was a good-natured, simple fellow, and had three main characteristics : he was inexacting, he was neat, and a home-bird. Moreover, he was no longer young, although he had not abandoned the hope that in case of need he could still stand up for himself. All his life he had worked in the Commissariat Department, had earned a major's rank, and there had educated his intellect and his heart. He did not take bribes (the reign of rapacity was over) but had succeeded by various shady little practices in amassing a tidy little fortune. Once he happened to get a bargain in a consignment of canary-seed and thought at once : ' I 'll marry a Canary and feed my wife and children on canary-seed ! ' His mother and father he had lost when still a fledgling, had inherited no patrimony, and was not slow therefore to inform his friends that he was indebted for his comfortable position to his own exertions. Even the accomplishment of carrying a little pail full of water was self-taught.

Such was the character and disposition of the bride-

groom. To be sure there was nothing specially pre-
disposing about him, but from the point of view of the
law he left nothing to be desired as an inhabitant.

His appearance too was in no way brilliant and striking ; on the contrary, this was extremely ordinary and
even humdrum. Even the Sparrows used to laugh,
when he wanted to pay a young lady a compliment, at
the way he used to shake his coat-tails and roll his eyes.
And his compliments, too, were such uninteresting ones:
he would tell some Commissariat anecdote, or boast that
however cheaply a cabman offered to drive him, he
would always give him five kopeks less, or if there was
time, would even walk.

' And so thanks be to God,' he would end up, ' I can
support not only myself, but a family also.'

Parents liked such sentiments, and tried so strenu-
ously to catch him in their toils that once they very
nearly choked him. But the daughters used to call him
' commissariat cholera,' and instantly scattered as soon
as he appeared, although their mammas commanded
them ' Restez ! ' But he, far from being offended by
these girlish tricks, would even comfort the parents,
saying :

' Never mind, ma'am, never mind. I am used to it.
When I was in the Commissariat Department there was
a little Wagtail. Such a charmer I may tell you—ah !
And from her too, at first, I heard nothing but " hee-
hee-hee," and " ha-ha-ha." I said to her : " Let us be
acquainted, mam'selle," and she, " Oh, no, you are
detestable." In a word, I made for her, she made off

from me, this way and that. Well, I got her at last.
And what do you think ? In the end she even praised
me for it ! '

' Dear me, Ivan Ivanovitch,' said the parents banter-
ingly, ' what a creature you are ! You haven't by any
chance any children " sur la main gauche " ? '

' I cannot say for certain, ma'am. I could not take
my oath on it. To natural weakness I have in my time
paid due tribute. I think of it this way : one should
not allow excess, but in moderation now, why not take
one's pleasures ? It 's the same with vodka. I don't
refuse it, but I don't drink myself blind—but " on due
occasion " as the song says.'

Of late years he had given up his Commissariat office.
' Saved enough, sir.' His wants were few, and the little
fortune God had sent him he had taken firm hold on.
So that ordinary interest was more than sufficient for
him, and at compound he would simply not know what
to do with his money. ' I get my clothing free,' he used
to say, ' given me by God—what I eat too. I do not
have to buy, but if I want entertainment, that too, sent
by God also, is inexpensive. I sing a song, and there I
am. Hence, while there are flies in the world, spiders,
worms, and other such provender, and while I have
strength to catch them, I am provided for. If my
strength leaves me, then I shall have to die. Well,
what matter ? It 's always so with other birds.'

If, while at work, his dearest dreams were of the
domestic hearth, the samovar, a dressing-gown, a double
bed, and of all such ideals born in the Commissariat

Department (for what is a bachelor, Siskin, he used to reflect : nothing but a medical term), on his resignation these thoughts began to depress him more and more. And so, having looked out a little yellow Canary, he donned his uniform, fastened on his spurs (all this he had received as a donation when he resigned), and set off to the parents of his intended to propose for her hand.

For the first time in his life exaltation took possession of his soul. For the first time in his life he sang ' Along the street, the broad-paved street,' and did not sing flat. A passion for the beautiful Canary so inundated his mind that, contrary to his usual cautious habits, he quite omitted to enquire what kind of bird his bride was, and whether she had a dowry.

And this perhaps would not have come amiss, as the bride was a cultivated young lady, used to the best society. She liked to have little airs and graces, to dress. She sang ' Si vous n'avez rien à me dire,' played ' le Ruisseau ' on the musical box, and was bored if she had no young men about her. She may have been kind-hearted, but she never had time to think of that. They would bring the new fashions from the shops, or her brother's friends from the military college would come in. And so, among her many occupations, she never noticed her kindness of heart.

' Mademoiselle, may I kiss your little foot ? ' the young military friends would pester her.

' Oh, you are . . . Well, kiss it then.'

And that was all.

Her parents were society people too, and like her they

were bored when there was no company. Her papa had for fifteen years been Marshal of the Nobility in the Canary Province, had run through four inheritances, sold his last serf certificates a year ago, and now lived on financial operations and got so nippy at it, that he used to give cab-drivers the slip through yard passages. As for mamma, as she had in her youth been a Canary, so in her old age a Canary she remained. She hopped from perch to perch, looked out for pleasant gentlemen, and remembered with gratitude how, when she was the Marshaless, she ate painted ginger-cakes, and the governor Peacock spread his tail at the sight of her. She brought up her eldest daughter on the same lines.

' I am not sending my little girl in for Higher Education,' she said to the Siskin, when he proposed. ' I think if a young girl knows French and how to hop from perch to perch, and dress becomingly and entertain— that 's all that 's necessary for a woman's happiness.'

' You have done very well, madam,' assented the Siskin, ' to have brought your daughter up in the fear of God. The male sex, to be sure, ought to have a knowledge of geography, because you never know when the Authorities may order you to fly off—and where, you know not. But a young lady any gentleman will be delighted to see on her way. All one needs is simply not to be led astray, that 's all.'

' Oh no, on that score you may be quite confident, major. My daughter is such a good, wise girl, that if she were to find herself in the depths of the forest with an Uhlan she would come to no harm.'

' So I hope, ma'am.'

Besides these three, the family consisted of a younger daughter and two sons. The younger daughter looked more like an unfledged Jackdaw than a Canary—her name was Galochka [1] too ; the eldest was called Proserpinochka—and so the parents looked down on her as a sort of Cinderella. But she was a kind girl, devoted to her family, and energetic, and in spite of the fact that every one ordered her about, treated her like a servant, and grudged her every bit she ate, she warmly loved her parents, her sister, and her brothers. The only thing she used to cry on the quiet about was that her household duties did not leave her time to go to University lectures. As for her brothers, the eldest was a cadet for an Uhlan regiment, and could not manage to pass his exam in Scripture, and the younger went to the High School and could never understand why the Authorities required him to know Greek.

' Now, what 's the good of that donkeyish language to me, mamma ? ' he complained to his mother. ' Now Latin there 's some sense in. " Mons parturiens mus . . . mons, montis ; mus, muris ; parturio, parturire, parturivi. . . ." Of course it might come in useful for writing prescriptions perhaps, or for quotations, or to shove some into a leading article. But Greek . . . Now what on earth is the good of Greek to me ? '

' Perhaps it 's for behaviour,' guessed the mother.

' Oh, mamma ! '

The whole day long in that house there was running

[1] Little crow.—*Tr.*

about, there were visitors and meals. They hopped
from perch to perch, they sang and played the musical
box. Canary-seed, fine birdseed, bread and milk,
mashed egg yolk, were perpetually on the table, and
yet they were owing to the general shop for this six
months past. The old Canary turned this way and that
like an eel in a frying-pan, trying to invent ways of
getting money. Every morning he flew round all his
acquaintance ; to one he would say that his aunt had
just died and he was in need of money to get his legacy ;
to another that on his land they had discovered coal, but
it could not be worked without capital ; to a third he
would simply announce that he was desperately in need
of cash. And sometimes he would come simply to one
of his cadet visitors and say, ' Have you got a twenty-
kopek piece about you, young man ? I will give it back
to you to-morrow with pleasure.' But they would have
their game too. The Uhlan cadets would come in,
drive Proserpinochka into a corner, and twirl their
moustaches. And poor Galochka, seeing what danger
her dear sister was in, would shed streams of tears.

Such was the family into which the Siskin made up his
mind to marry. All the neighbours knew that the old
Canary was bankrupt, that the mamma Canary had been
seen only the other day whispering in the bushes with
the shopkeeper Thrush, that Proserpinochka herself,
under cover of taking singing lessons, used to go and see
the Nightingale, and that afterwards—so people said—
she had laid a wind egg. . . . But the Siskin seemed to
have gone blind and deaf. Having received the parents'

163

consent, in rapture he flew from tree to tree trying to catch a sight of his lovely bride bathing in the bird bath, and when he succeeded, he would burst into song. He sang very loud and very flat, but alas, this was his only means of giving thanks to the Creator for these the blessings of his life.

'I know and feel,' he said, 'that this grace vouchsafed to me is above my station, but I will endeavour to earn the same in the future.'

However, in fairness to Proserpinochka, it must be said that she never attempted to disguise her indifference to the Siskin. When her parents announced that the major had done her the honour of proposing for her hand, and that they had already given their consent, she was instantly seized with a fit of laughing and said :

'Oh, mamma, do just look how awfully funny he is ! '

And then, when the parents left them alone together on purpose, so that they should get to know each other better, instead of compliments there ensued between them this rather frank conversation :

'Are you stingy ? ' Proserpinochka asked him.

'I am not stingy, miss, but saving,' the Siskin answered. 'I think of it this way—why should one throw money about, when one can live on what one has ? But for you, I am ready even to abandon my saving habits.'

With these words the major gallantly clicked his heels together, but alas—this not only failed to touch Proserpinochka's heart, but on the contrary, only called forth a fresh burst of merriment.

'Oh, how awfully amusing you are when you click

your heels ! Do it again, again. That 's right. Ha-ha-ha ! Well, what do you have to eat at home ? Some nasty mess ? '

' For my own self, I eat food given me by God—simple but wholesome. But for you I will get canary-seed.'

' Oh no, I like salad best.'

' Oh, I can get you salad if it comes to that. I will fly off to a kitchen garden early in the morning and pick some. Some people would run themselves into a deal of expense over that, but I 'll get it for you for nothing.'

' Well, then, what will you give me for a present ? They sent some new-fashioned cuffs from Paris the other day. . . . Will you give me some ? Will you ? '

' With the very greatest pleasure. I 'll give the spider the order this very day, to be ready first thing to-morrow.'

' Yes, but cuffs like that are very expensive. . . .'

' Don't trouble about that, miss. When the spider comes to me for the money, I 'll simply eat him—and we 'll be quits.'

' Ha-ha-ha ! How awfully funny you are ! '

And so it went on. She never said ' Darling ' to her fiancé, or ' pet ' : ' Awfully funny,' and that was all. She was scarcely ever with him, but surrounded herself with cadets and schoolboys and held whispered conversations with them in the most shameless manner.

' Do you know, major, what they told me about you ? ' she would say to him point-blank : ' that in the last war you fed the army and the fleet with rotten biscuits.'

165

He would grow confused, but would not deny it, for although biscuits were not in his department, his conscience was not quite clear—he used to adulterate hay for the army horses, and that perhaps was a bit worse—for a soldier can at any rate complain, but a horse has no words to complain with.

Ah, he did ill, then!

And sometimes Proserpinochka made game of him before the whole company. The young people would be playing a game of 'Fire!' for instance, and he like a fool would be hanging around too. So they would make him 'the one in the fire,' and blindfold him too. He would dash forward to catch them, spread his wings, fly along—and she and her friends the cadets would hide in the bushes. They would peep out and call 'Catch us, major, catch us!' until he went bang into a pine trunk.

At first the old Canary used to be afraid that the major might be offended, and called out from time to time to her daughter, 'Finissez!' But when she saw that it was like water off a duck's back, she made no more efforts, and only asked him every evening regularly, 'Do you happen to have a rouble on you, major? We will give it back to you to-morrow with pleasure.'

Galochka alone pitied the poor Siskin, and who knows whether a more tender sentiment did not take part in the pity? At any rate, once, when the major, flapping his wings lazily, was returning home late one night, Galochka caught him up.

'Now, is it suitable for you to love a beautiful creature

like that?' she said to him. ' You had much better marry me. I would look after you so well.'

But he was simply struck dumb. He did not even stop to hear properly what Galochka was saying, and answered rudely :

' If I had wanted to marry a Jackdaw I should have proposed for a Jackdaw. But as I proposed for your sister, it 's obvious that it 's her I wish to have to do with.'

And yet it cannot be said that he understood nothing. On the contrary, he understood a great deal, with great subtlety. But at the same time he saw that it was all up with him and that his fate was sealed irrevocably and for ever. Why for ever, he could not himself have told, but only kept repeating : ' Irrevocably and for ever ! '

And so he got married. After the wedding they feasted the whole evening, so that the night was far spent when the Siskin turned towards his nest with his young wife. It was lovely, glorious ! The warm night was fragrant, the stars in the deep blue of heaven shone like diamonds, and the Siskin burned as if on fire. Rapture coursed through his veins—glorious, intoxicating rapture ! He did not know whether he wanted to sing or to sob, yet a sensitive delicacy bade him restrain his impulses. It seemed as if Proserpinochka herself had fallen under the spell of his passion. Languishingly she closed her eyes, and with a delicious tremor passing through her frame, gave him a little peck on the top of his head. But at that instant a drunken band passed the opening of the Siskin's hollow in his tree. It was her brothers with a whole crowd of boon companions. With yells and shrieks they were shouting out the song : ' Malbourg s'en va-t-en guerre.' On hearing these sounds the young bride was instantly transformed. In her night deshabille she ran out to the edge of the hollow in their tree and till late cock-crow stood giggling with the cadets. The Siskin, having donned his uniform, came up behind his young wife and tried to make merry also. But alas !—he speedily came to the conclusion that merriment does not suit a major. Try as he would, his position, and his advancing years, together got the better of him. His eyes closed of their own accord, and in another moment loud snores filled the hollow of the tree trunk. Even the burst of laughter which followed did not awake him. So, in uniform, buttoned up to the neck, he spent his honeymoon.

From this moment he was finally lost in the eyes of his wife.

When he awoke—although it was still very early— Proserpinochka was already gone. The little Linnet whom he had got for a maid announced that ' Miss Proserpine ' had gone home to mamma and did not know whether she would be back to dinner. ' *Miss* Proserpine ! ' At that word he recoiled as if he had been scalded.

He peeped out of the hollow and hopped on to the nearest branch. All around absolute stillness reigned : the stillness just before awakening when all Nature seems dead. The birds had not awakened, even the leaves on the trees did not stir. But the East was reddening, and it seemed to the major that rosy-fingered Aurora with an ironic greeting was making him a long nose. Evidently something of grave importance in his life had happened that night, something that would be like an irretrievable blot on his whole future existence. He had some duty to perform—a very simple one, to be sure, and natural to every Siskin—but he, like the wicked and slothful servant, failed to fulfil it.

Considering the matter from every point of view, he first of all prevaricated. Or, to put it in scientific language, he began to consider the subject from its root causes. Did the failure in his duty spring from circumstances over which he had control, or did it not ? 'If I had really been the cause of this mishap—then indeed ! If it is my fault, take my head, and I 'll say nothing. But really, there is not the slightest blame attaching to me—and yet look what has happened now ! ' But no sooner had he invented this excuse than he understood its futility. There are facts to which the law of causation is inapplicable. They have to be realised, and no brain-twisting will re-create that which *should have been* and *was not*. Not one young husband, not one loving mother, not one court of jury or Crown court will bring in any other verdict than ' shame, shame, shame ! '

He should have repulsed the attack of the drunken company, he should have made his nest impregnable, he should with his manly breast have defended his right to fulfil his 'duty,' he should, in the name of duty, have entered into mortal combat. . . . 'Qu'il mourit!'

'Shame, sir!' he repeated mechanically, and mechanically, without even changing his uniform, dishevelled as he was, he flew off *there*.

The old Canary was already awake, and as cross as cross. Besides the fact that her Proserpinochka had suffered this 'shame,' that night a Canary cousin had come to visit her from three-times-nine lands away, and finally goaded her to desperation with her tales. She also had her Darling in marriage, to a Bullfinch; but oh, what a difference!

'How he loves my Darling,' said her visitor; 'how he loves her! C'est tout un poème. . . . Imagine. . . .'

The visitor bent down to her cousin's ear, whispered something, and then with delighted horror leant back, repeating:

'But just imagine my precious one's astonishment!!!'

And the old Canary listened and spitefully ground her beak.

'Well, well, may God give your Darling . . . may God . . .' she whispered. 'And we . . . some people have luck, and we . . . See what joy her husband brings your Darling, and we . . . You would think Proserpinochka would be the last to be called scraggy. . . . She is plump, and lively, her cheeks and her breast . . . And what do you think? Didn't so much as notice them—the scoundrel!'

'Est-ce possible?'

At that very moment the Siskin appeared. He just opened his mouth to justify himself, when the outraged mother-in-law, pointing to the door, cried :

' Sortez ! Shame, sir ! Shame, shame, shame ! '

And after her the cousin repeated like an echo :

' Shame, shame, shame ! '

Overwhelmed, he wanted to fly wherever his wings would take him, but his wings seemed as if they had been broken. He took the road which led to his nest, thinking there to hide his shame, but the birds were already awake and knew all. And although not one of them made any ' suitable ' allusion to his face, and some even came up and congratulated him, he could see quite plainly that in the eyes of each one was written :

' Shame, shame, shame ! '

In the evening, however, Proserpinochka returned, but without saying ' bon jour,' flew straight into her nest.

' My darling, my pet, my angel ! ' the Siskin whistled after her, and so mournfully, that the Linnet, though a bird of humble birth, was moved to tears.

But Proserpinochka answered not a sound, and the Siskin only heard her scratching up the down in her nest with her little feet, preparing her bed for the night.

' My wife, given me by God ! ' cried the major, with not so much a whistle as a kind of howl, and burst into tears.

But even that appeal did not move Proserpinochka, He came up to her bed and bent over her, but she was already asleep, or more probably pretended to be.

So this night too the major had to spend in solitude. His coat, of course, he took off, but did not venture to take off his trousers for fear of embarrassing Proserpinochka. And next morning, early as he awoke, Proserpinochka was already gone—she had again flown off to her parents.

The major's martyrdom began.

In the course of a whole month his young wife did not exchange a single word with him. Every night she came to the Siskin's hollow tree, went to bed in her nest, and every morning disappeared so mysteriously and adroitly that the major could never catch her. Some four times she came in company with a crowd of cadets and schoolboys, called the Linnet to her, and ordered a sumptuous supper. But she and her companions ate and drank before the Siskin's eyes in the most shameless manner and did not once so much as say thank you to him, just as if, instead of being the master of his hollow, he was some caretaker. In his wife's family he was invariably referred to as ' the scoundrel.'

' The scoundrel has bought a lottery ticket again,' the old Canary informed her cousin, who was making a prolonged stay.

Or :

' I think " the scoundrel " will go out of his mind soon. He has begun to be very thoughtful.'

His old father-in-law alone used to come and see the major now and again, to say comforting things

to him, and even promised to give Proserpinochka
a whipping, but never fulfilled his promise, and only
got a whole heap of twenty-kopek pieces out of the
major.

Another month passed. Proserpinochka's relations
with the major underwent a change, but not for the
better. The Canary in her came out—she became
brazen. She acted the mute no longer, but spoke to the
Siskin in the tone of voice which a queen uses to some
obscure stoker in her palace.

'Money,' she would demand.

'How much, my dear?'

'Not "how much"—just give it to me.'

Neither how much nor what it was for would she so
much as mention. She may have behaved so on purpose, wishing to cut the Siskin to the heart, or she may
have done it unthinkingly. Who knows? A Canary's
soul is unfathomable, and not a single wise man can dis-
entangle within it where the graceful flutter of thought
ends, and where begins the wish to torture. Be that as
it may, the Siskin never refused her. He used to go
into the back room of the hollow for a minute, and with
trembling hands bring out his money-box. And while
she idly scooped up the silver five-kopek pieces from
the heap, smiling strangely the while, he felt as if
his soul were being dragged out of him. Not because
he was stingy, but he had an innate necessity to
know the precise state of his exchequer at any given
moment.

Having robbed her husband's exchequer, she would

173

fly off, and in another hour he would see the results of the robbery. Proserpinochka at the head of a whole band of Uhlans and society ladies of light behaviour with noise and singing would fly by, and alight in the nearest meadow. There they would have a merry picnic at the Siskin's expense, and the whole gang feasted, sang, and danced far into the night, and from time to time scattered into the bushes for repose.

One evening Proserpinochka came home in an unusually excited state. She flew about the hollow (nearly hit her little breast !), whirled round and round, sang, laughed and cried. . . . The major observed her first with consternation, then dotingly. Unfortunately it occurred to him that Proserpinochka's heart had been melted, that his suffering was at an end, that she was coming to meet him half-way . . . coming to fill him with bliss, endless bliss ! A sweet poignant agitation filled his whole being and woke in him a boldness not to be found in every major from the Commissariat Department. In the heat of his passion he stole up to Proserpinochka just when, standing at the opening of the hollow, she was gazing into the dark void beyond, and gave her a soft peck on the top of her head.

'Idiot !' she cried out, and evading his embrace, flew out of the hollow.

This was a decisive step on her part. Up till then she had always gone off for the day, now she had gone off for the night !

So passed a whole fortnight. At night—mysterious disappearance ; in the day—hysterics, tears. The

174

major was worn out with suffering. He followed her about, carrying a little pail of water in his beak in case she felt faint, and implored her tearfully :

' Have a little water, darling. Tell me what is the matter. Not as to your husband, alas, I have not deserved that happiness—as to a father, a brother ! Who has been unkind to you, my little pet ? '

' Idiot ! ! ! ! '

At last she did not come back at all. The major waited a day, waited another, and then resolved . . . to wait indefinitely. A sad time this was for him—a time of complete loneliness. His wife had left him ; her relations, without a word, had disappeared—the old Canary must really have got a legacy from his aunt ; and he was ashamed to look the other birds in the face, because he still had not expiated his shame, had not justified himself. Even their maid, the Linnet, gave notice and built a nest with a Sparrow in some garret.

Up till now he had at any rate suffered—suffered acutely, poignantly. These sufferings had made him convulsively fling himself to and fro, made him cry out, curse . . . and hope ; now these sufferings had taken a dull, passive form, which paralysed his actions, chained his will, and filled his future with impenetrable darkness. . . .

Meanwhile the autumn was coming on. The birds began to fuss around their nests ; he alone did nothing, irresolute as to whether to fly to the warm springs, or to remain in his native country. The rains began, and

cold winds ; the woods, now bare, made a dismal noise,
the nights grew long and dark. And he, whole nights
together, hungry and cold, sat at the entrance of his
hollow and waited. How many times the murderous
Owl flew by, just missing his hollow with her wing !
How many times the bloodthirsty Weasel peeped into
his hole ! But, by a happy chance, neither the Owl nor
the Weasel disturbed him. Perhaps from the point of
view of edibility he was now too meagre, but perhaps
too the rapacious creatures knew what an able official of
the Commissariat he had been in his time, and not wishing to deprive their country of his services in the future,
spared him. . . .

Understanding that his life was shattered, his
thoughts instinctively turned to the past. So clean,
neat, well-ordered this had been, the Siskin's heart rejoiced. And not without its pleasant incidents either.
Not only the Commissariat enterprises. But, for instance, the Wagtail. What a sharp, natty little girl
that was . . . crisp as a little cucumber. And she too at
first used to laugh : ' Oh, how awfully funny you are ! '
Funny and funny, and then all of a sudden : ' Oh,
darling, what a little silly I was—just wasted the time
for nothing ! ' He should have married her, and he
went and left her with six children. Or again—he had
turned in to an inn beside the highway kept by a little
widow, Quail, who did a trade in millet-seed and
buckwheat too. A word after another : ' How much
is your millet ? What 's the grain ? I expect it 's
sad for you without your husband, ma'am . . .' and

176

on a sudden the lights all went out. . . . Her too he should have married, and he promised—and then made off !

Oh, it was lovely then—glorious ! The more heartlessly he treated the Wagtails and the Quails in those days, the prouder he was of himself, the more praises he heard. All the Commissariat clerks used to say of him, ' Our major is a regular dog. . . . There he goes making up to them, there he goes a-swaggering. Serve them right, the silly little idiots !

Ah—should he not go back to the Commissariat ? Why not ? Take pen and paper, write an application— they would take him, take him with pleasure.

But scarcely had the thought occurred to him than he impatiently dismissed it. It was not of Wagtails and little Quails he had to think now—no ! Henceforth there was only one thing for him—to suffer acutely and to wait. To wait for his priceless little yellow young lady, his God-given wife ! She would come back— she would for sure !

There were times, however, when he rebelled. Not of his own accord, but under the influence of evil birds who came to him to borrow money. The most pernicious influence in that respect was exerted on him by the Blackbird. He always began by expressing his sympathy for the Siskin's loneliness, and then very astutely hinted that in these times it was the easiest thing to get a divorce.

' Hire a lawyer-chap,' he used to say, ' and the whole thing 's done ! The lawyer will polish it off for you in an hour ! Do get divorced, old man. What 's the good of considering her, the slut ! '

Besides the Blackbird, the Chaffinch used to work him up, but the Chaffinch was against divorce and advised the Siskin to send in a petition to the District Police Office.

' It 's doing them too much honour, getting divorced from every slut like that,' he used to say. ' Go straight to the District Police Office—they 'll give her such a doing there as she won't forget till the new besoms are made ! '

And one fine day the major fell a prey to the temptation. He flew off to Petersburg, and went straight to the lawyer Balalaikin.

' I want to marry a wife when I 've one living—work it,' he said.

' With pleasure,' answered Balalaikin. ' I myself have run through four wives living and am married to a fifth, and as you see have not been in prison even.'

But from the Balalaikin's tone alone the Siskin understood that no good would come of his efforts. Having paid Balalaikin twenty kopeks (for nothing but lies), with a heavy heart he flew to the District Office, but there too he suffered a reverse.

' Bring her here and we will whip her,' they said very reasonably. ' But if you go on troubling us uselessly, we will lay you out yourself, major though you are.'

This was, so to speak, the last effort of rebellious flesh. He returned home finally subdued.

The winter went by. Half-frozen, famished, scarcely alive, the Siskin crept out of his hollow and just managed to make his way to the river. The ice was so far thawed that in places there were already pools. He approached one of them in the hope of picking up some old thing to eat, but seeing his reflection in the water, he uttered a cry of dismay. During the winter he had grown so thin, so meagre and bony, that his uniform hung on him as on a coat-hanger. There was no trace of the former neatly buttoned, clean, well-fed little Siskin. Even his spurs had disappeared, goodness knows where. With pain at his heart he returned to the hollow, and from that moment finally lost all faith in a brighter future.

What use even if he lived to see her come back? How could he greet her? What proof could he offer her of faithful, loving marital devotion?

And suddenly one warm May night *she* came back. She came back ill, thin, dishevelled, and somehow *not herself*. The little crest on her head had been plucked out, her wing feathers crumpled, her tail was thin, even her little yellow dress had faded and gone greyish. And she shook all over, whether with cold or with shame he could not tell. The Siskin scarcely knew her.

' Well, here I am ! ' she said.

' Come in, then,' the Siskin answered.

That was all the conversation that passed between them. Of the past—not a word ; of the future—not a syllable.

And so from that moment they lived side by side in the same hollow, silently, always thinking about something. Perhaps they awaited a miracle which should open their hearts and fill them with the joy of forgiveness and love ; but perhaps they confessed themselves finally crushed and gloomily lamented : he—' Ah, how you have broken my life, you heartless doll ! ' and she : ' Ah, how you have wrecked my youth, you hateful major ! '

KRAMÓLNIKOV'S[1] MIS-
ADVENTURE

(*An Elegy*)

ONCE, on waking in the morning, Kramólnikov quite
clearly felt that he did not exist. Only yesterday he
was aware that he *was* ; to-day, yesterday's *being* in
some mysterious manner had changed into *non-being*.
But this non-being was of a particular kind. Kramólnikov hastily felt himself all over, then said a few words
aloud, then looked into the glass : it appeared that he
was there, he was all there, and that as a census unit he
still existed exactly as he had the day before.

Not only this : he tried to think—and it appeared
that he could think. . . . And yet, in spite of all this, there
was no doubt that he did not exist. The Kramólnikov
who was not a census unit—that Kramólnikov had
ceased to be. It was as if some door had banged to
behind him, or the road in front of him had become
impassable, and he had nowhere to go, and no object
in going.

Turning from one supposition to another, and at the
same time observing his surroundings with curiosity, he
happened to glance at the literary work he had begun,
which lay on his table, and suddenly through his whole
being an electric current ran piercingly :

' Useless, useless, useless ! '

---

[1] Kramolnik = rebel. —*Tr.*

At first he thought 'What nonsense!' and took up his pen. But as soon as he tried to continue his work, he was convinced that he ought to draw a line, and under it to write 'Useless!'

He understood that all was as before—only that his soul was locked up. Henceforth he was free to exercise the spirit proper to a census unit; he was free perhaps even to think; but it was all useless. He had lost that which had made the sense and substance of his life, he had lost that luminous force which had enabled him with the fire of his heart to light the hearts of others. He stood amazed; he looked and did not see, he sought and did not find. Something intensely painful burned him within. . . . And in the air, meantime, floated an absurdly provocative whisper, 'We 've found you out! we 've nosed it out! We' ve got you!'

'What is it, what has happened?'

His soul was undoubtedly sealed up. Like all men who have a faith and principles, Kramólnikov possessed an inner shrine, in which he kept the treasure of his soul. He did not hide the treasure, he did not consider it his exclusive property. But in it, he felt, lay the whole meaning of man's life. Without this active force, human society would become a graveyard—this force which gives man the urge to shed upon his fellows light and good, and at the same time endows him with the ability to receive light and good from others. It would be no longer society, but a pile of corpses. . . . And now the corpse period had begun for him. The interchange of the force of light and good had come to an end.

Kramólnikov himself was a corpse, and all to whom he turned but lately as to a source of living water for his activity—they too were corpses. . . . Never had he even remotely imagined so appalling a disaster.

Kramólnikov was a veritable Poshekhónie [1] man of letters. He had no affections save for his reader, no joys but being in touch with the reader. The reader did not materialise for him in any particular form, yet nevertheless was constantly before him. In this attachment to an abstract personality there was something unusual, almost morbidly passionate. For years it alone sustained him, and with every year it became more and more insistent. At length came old age, and to all life's blessings save one—the highest and the most important—he became indifferent, he had no need of them.

And suddenly at this moment the last blessing crashed also. A black abyss opened before him, swallowing that ' sole thing ' which gave his life meaning.

In the literary world one sometimes meets with natures thus exclusively directed. From early youth their lives form so one-sided a bent, that whatever chance push them from the fateful rut, the deflection is never serious or lasting. Under the heaps of accumulated rubbish the true stream of life still flows. All the variety of life seems unreal ; all its interest is concentrated on a single point of light. They never think

---

[1] Poshekhónie, a division of the Yaroslav goubernia—a district with a reputation of extreme backwardness, and its inhabitants a by-word for stupidity. Shchedrin frequently uses the name for Russia as a whole.— *Tr.*

what chance awaits them on life's way, they never look
ahead, nor plan defences in their rear, nor recon-
noitre, nor make comparisons with occurrences in the
past. This not because they do not understand the
significance of events before their eyes, but because no
forethought, no investigation can alter one iota of that
function the cessation of which would be the cessation of
being. You would have to kill the man to end the
function.

Was it possible that this murder had now taken place,
at this mysterious moment ? What had happened ?
Vainly he tried to find an answer to this question. He
understood only that a gaping void surrounded him
on every side.

Kramólnikov warmly and passionately loved his
country and had a thorough knowledge both of its present
and of its past. But this knowledge had upon him an
unusual effect ; it was a living source of perpetual pain,
which became in time the chief content of his life, and
gave colour and direction to all his work. He did not
try to lessen this pain, but on the contrary did his best
to keep it living in his heart. The acuteness of this pain,
its ceaselessness, served as a creative source of living
images with the aid of which it was communicated to
others.

He knew that the country of Poshekhónie was of old
famous for its inconstancy and instability, that Nature
itself seemed there somehow to merit only distrust.
Its rivers, flowing wide, each year changed their course,
leaving innumerable dry sandy beds. The atmospheric

changes were astoundingly sudden, as if by magic to-day it would seem to be hot—you could wring out your shirt, —to-morrow the same shirt would be like a board upon your back. The summer was short, the vegetation poor, and marshlands stretched as far as eye could reach. . . . In short, Nature there was unprepossessing, treacherous, such as did not encourage the planning of work ahead.

Still more uncertain in Poshekhónie is the fate of man. The riff-raff say, ' The beggar's scrip and prison there is no escaping.' The peasant says, ' The sum of our profits is written on the water with a pitchfork.' The nobleman says, ' Yesterday I had ears higher than my forehead, and to-day I cannot even find them.' There is nothing to connect yesterday with to-morrow ! Man wanders in the Vale of Chance : if God sees him through, he is a lord ; if God does not, he is done for.

What question can there be of conscience when all about one is treacherous, betrays ? On what can conscience rest ? What will educate it ?

Kramólníkov knew all this, but as I said before, this knowledge only made the pain in his heart the livelier, and served as an impetus for his activity. He deeply loved his country, loved its poverty, its nakedness, its lucklessness. Perhaps he saw before it in the future a miracle which should stay the grief with which it was consumed.

He believed in miracles and awaited them. Brought up in the midst of magic, imperceptibly to himself he submitted to the magic and acknowledged it as the decisive factor in the life of Poshekhónie. In what direction would the magic exert its force—that was the question. . . . Moreover, the past had not always been all blackness. Now and again the darkness had cleared a little, and during those intervals the Poshekhónians undoubtedly had had more vigour. This faculty of taking courage and of becoming vigorous, as it were of flowering under the rays of the sun, however feeble, proves that light is a desirable thing for men in general. This instinctive thirst for the light should be sustained in them ; they should be reminded that life is joy, and not everlasting suffering from which death is the only release. It is not death which must break the bonds, but the restored image of man, clear-cut and freed from those indignities with which ages of the slavery of a beast of burden had covered it. So clearly does this truth appear from the study of human nature that it is impossible to entertain a doubt of its ultimate triumph. Kramólnikov believed in this triumph, and gave himself wholly to the task of keeping this belief before men's minds.

The whole force of his mind and of his heart he consecrated to the work of maintaining in the souls of his fellow-men the faith that light would come and darkness could not vanquish it. In that lay the whole end and aim of his activity.

And indeed the magic was not long in claiming its rights. But not the beneficent magic of which he dreamt, but the ordinary cruel magic of Poshekhónie.

Useless ! Useless ! Useless !

186

To Kramólnikov's honour, be it said, he did not once ask himself ' Why ? How did I deserve this ? ' He understood that in the complete absence of any cause this kind of question was not only out of place, but would even be merely evidence of weakness of character. He did not deny that it was entirely normal—this that had befallen him ; he only held that his normal state had declared itself too cruelly, too sharply. More than once had it fallen to his lot to play the part of *anima vitis* before the magic power, but up till now it had at least left his soul untouched. Now it had seized this soul, crumpled it, imprisoned it, and familiar as Kramólnikov was with the vagaries of the magic power, this time he was overwhelmed. His whole being seemed broken, and he felt all through him an intense and wholly unfamiliar pain.

And suddenly he thought of 'the reader.' Up to this moment he had given to the reader all his powers unthinkingly : but now a faint perception of an answering voice, of sympathy, of help, stirred in him for the first time. . . .

Instinctively he felt a need to go out, as if there, in the street, some explanation awaited him.

The street had the usual Poshekhónian air. To Kramólnikov it seemed that before his eyes extended dumb, blind, deaf space. Only the stones cried out. Men scurried to and fro, cautiously, casting suspicious glances all about them, as if they were going to thieve. This was the only spark of life. All else seemed, as it were, to be dumbfounded, to be stricken with stupefaction. However, Kramólnikov at first thought that even this dumb street *knew* something. He had such an intense desire for this, that the cry of the stones he took for the cry of men. Still he was not altogether wrong. There was indeed, here and there, an incoherent buzzing. This was the buzzing of the Liberals, his sometime friends. Some he passed, others he met. But alas! not one flicker of sympathy did he see in their faces. On the contrary, the shadow of apostasy lay on them now.

' Well, they 've buried you pretty quick, my dear sir ! ' one said. ' It 's a sharp rap, a sharp rap ! But then, you know, you did . . . It won't do. I told you long ago it wouldn't do ! They stood you and stood you, and at last . . .'

' And what " at last " ? '

' Why, simply at last—and that 's all. They had had enough. Now is the time, not for talking, but for looking on—and, when possible, for perceiving. You should have known yourself, my dear sir ; if you did not want to conform wholeheartedly, you might at any rate have done it tentatively—find out what I am like . . . inside ! But you go at it straight from the shoulder ! Well, of course they had soon had enough. And I, you know—do you think I have an easy time of it ? You have known me some time. But I have thought and thought, sought people's advice. . . . God have mercy on us—in we plunge ! '

Another said, ' Yes, my friend, I am sorry for you— very. It was pleasant to read you. One smiles, sighs,

and now and again finds something of importance. . . .
Even hastens to tell one's friends of it. You were
quoted in government offices. I had a friend who knew
quite a lot by heart. But on the other hand there *are*
limits. The time has come when there is need of something different ; you should have understood that, and
not waited till you were shut down. What this " something else " is, will appear later, but not just now. . . .
I kept looking where other people were going, and said
to my wife, " Yes, I must." And she said too, " You
must." So I made up my mind.'

' Made up your mind to what ? '

' Why, simply to the general thorny path. No looking to the side, no soaring upward, no thinking of great
problems. . . . Gently and easily. . . . It 's dull, of course,
and colourless, but then, on the one hand, it is not for the
little people to be brilliant, on the other—the family.
My wife likes to dress, you know, have an entertaining
time. . . . And then for oneself too—there is one's position to think of, connections, acquaintances, one sees
other people getting up in the world—is it fair to lose
everything ? But don't think I shall be like this for
ever. . . . No, this is with a reservation. Better times
will come. . . . For instance, if Nikolai Semenich . . .
After all, one must live. . . . To-day it 's Ivan Mikhaelich
—to-morrow Nikolai Semenich. . . . Then we can
again . . .'

' But Nikolai Semenich is a thief ! '

' A thief ! Oh, what expressions you use ! '

Finally a third called out to him directly : ' Serve you

right! You 've done enough, sir. You compromise not only yourself, but others also. Why, yesterday I had to have an " explanation " all because of you, and to-day I don't know whether I am alive or dead. What right have you, I should like to know ? " You are, I think," he says, "on terms of friendship with Mr.Kramólnikov and therefore . . ." I tried this and that. " How can you call them terms of friendship, your Excellency ? Just a buffoon—why, after a day's work, not have a good laugh ? " Well, they have given me twenty-four hours for reflection—then Heaven only knows ! And I have a family, my dear sir, a wife and children. . . . And I myself am not exactly chaff in a field. Could one ever have thought of such a thing ! I say again—what right have you ? Oh, dear, dear, dear ! '

Kramólnikov did not choose to continue the conversation and went on his way. But as he passed a house in which an old schoolfellow of his lived, he turned in, thinking here at any rate to find consolation.

The footman received him hospitably ; evidently he did not know anything as yet. He said that Dmitry Nikolaich was out, but that Aglaia Alexéyevna was in the drawing-room. Kramólnikov opened the door, but hardly had he crossed the threshold, when the lady in the room screamed and ran away. Kramólnikov retreated.

At last he remembered that in the Pesky quarter lived an old colleague of his (Kramólnikov, some fifteen years ago, had also worked in the Ministry of Sinful Reflections), Jacov Ilych Voróboushkin.

He was a great admirer of Kramólnikov, and a man who was not successful in his career. More than ten years he had slaved at routine work as head clerk, having no hope of promotion, and at each change of political atmosphere trembled lest he lose his post. Timid and wanting in push, he could not make a success of private work. From the very first he had managed to establish himself in such a way that it seemed to him odd to try and obtain anything, to hand in memoranda suggesting men's dismissal or removal, to hang about superiors' front staircases, and so on. Once only had he handed in a memorandum about giving encouragement to the poor in spirit : but the director, having read it, only shook his finger at him, and this finally silenced Voróboushkin. Lately, however, his hopes had begun vaguely to rise ; he had begun to go to the same church as his chief, who even once gave him a present of half a communion-bread (the bottom half) and said, ' I am very pleased ! ' So that his affairs were on the mend, when suddenly . . .

The door was opened to Kramólnikov by the old nurse, and from the back, through the inner door, looked out children's frightened faces. The nurse was cross because the unexpected guest had interrupted her in the occupation of catching fleas. She said sharply to Kramólnikov, ' Jacov Ílych is out. He has been summoned to the Head because of you, and whether he is alive now or dead we don't know ; and the missus has gone to church.'

Kramólnikov began to descend the stairs, but he had

scarcely gone a few steps when he met Voróboushkin himself.

'Kramólnikov—forgive me—but I cannot continue our former relations,' said Voróboushkin in an agitated tone. 'This time I think I have cleared myself, but even of that I am not certain. The Director said, "There is an ineffaceable stain upon you!" And I have a wife and children! Leave me, Kramólnikov! Forgive me for being so poor-spirited. I cannot . . .'

Kramólnikov went home depressed, almost frightened. That henceforth he was condemned to loneliness he realised. He was solitary, not because he had no reader who valued, and who even perhaps loved him, but because he had lost all touch with *his* reader. This reader was far away and could not break the tie between them. But there was another, near him, who had the power to hurt Kramólnikov mortally at any time. He was still left, and insolently made it clear that Kramólnikov's very dumbness was hateful to him.

Dimly it passed through his mind, that in all the apostasies he had ever witnessed it was not personal treachery that played the important part but a whole depressing chain of events. He saw that these bold thinkers of yesterday, who but a short time ago shook hands with him so warmly, and to-day shunned him like the plague, did this not only from fear but because they were crushed.

They were crushed by their desire for life, but as the desire for life is entirely legitimate and natural, Kramólnikov was filled with fear at the thought. 'Must one

then,' he asked himself, ' in order to retain the right to
existence, must one pass through a cruel and shameful
slavery ? Is in this mysterious world only that natural
which goes counter to the dearest and most sacred
aspirations of the soul ? '

Or again : almost every one of his interlocutors justified himself by reference to his family ; one said ' my
wife likes to dress well,' the other ' my wife ' and no
more. . . . But the most saddening was from Voróboushkin. His family rent his heart. He probably
denied himself everything, ate too little, slept too little,
obtained extra work—all for the sake of his family.
And in spite of this he earned so little that only the self-
sacrifice of Loukeria Vassilievna (Voróboushkin's wife)
made this poverty bearable. And now, for this mite,
for a beggarly extra . . .

What was it then ? What is the family ? How
should we deal with that problem ? How can one
arrange things so that a family should not be a burden
to a man, so that it should not continually harass him
or prevent his being a citizen ?

Kramólnikov thought and thought, and suddenly
something seemed to pierce him through. ' Why,' said
an inner voice, ' why did these burning questions not
rise so insistently *before* as they do now ? Is it not
because you were a slave before, but knowing at any
rate that you had some force—and now you are a powerless, oppressed slave ? Why did you not go boldly
ahead and sacrifice yourself ? Why did you give yourself in bondage to a profession which yielded you a

position, influence, friends, instead of hastening where you heard moans ? Why did you not face those from whom these moans came instead of letting them move you only as abstractions ?

' From your pen flowed words of protest, but clothed in a form which made it moribund. All that you attacked still stands.

' Your labour has been fruitless. It was the labour of a barrister whose tongue is hopelessly involved in the net of lies surrounding him. You made your protest, but you have never shown what should be done, nor how men fell and were destroyed, you simply sent them words of sympathy, it was a captive's irritated, goaded thought—and nothing more. Even those who turned from you so brutally to-day, even them you failed to understand. You thought that *yesterday* and *to-day* their nature was different.

' You are incapable, it is true, of doing as these people do. You are incapable of being false to those goaded thoughts which from your youth have grown to be a part of you.

' This will of course be counted to your credit, where and when ? But now, when everywhere you look you see old age with all its ills come closing in upon you— what have you left ? '

.   .   .   .

Postscript from the Author.

Needless to say, all the preceding is nothing but a story. There 's no Kramólnikov, and there never was ;

apostates and turncoats there have always been, not only at this moment. And as in every other respect also all is entirely well, it was not worth while to make this fuss, for which the author sincerely begs the reader's forgiveness.

THE SUPPLIANT CROW

THE old crow's heart was well-nigh worn out with aching. The crow tribe was almost exterminated—any old lazybones had a shot at them. And if it had been for profit even—but no, it was just for amusement.

The crows themselves had got poor-spirited. There was not a trace of the old ill-omened cawing. They would just pitch on a birch-tree, a whole lot of them, and yell ' Here we are ! ' out of sheer foolishness. Naturally ' biff ! '—and there would be a dozen or two fewer in the flock in a moment. The free provender of old days, that was gone too. The forests round were cut down, the marshes drained, the beasts chased away—you couldn't pick up an honest living anyhow. And the crow tribe began to look about in gardens and farmyards and such places. And for this—biff again, and another dozen or two gone ! It's a good thing that crows are a prolific race, or else who would there have been left to pay tribute to the hawk and to the kite ?

The old crow would begin admonishing his younger brethren, ' Don't caw without need ! Don't hang about other people's gardens,' and hear only one reply, ' You don't know anything about ways nowadays, old dodderer ! You can't but thieve these times. Even science says the same : if you 've nothing to eat, live by your wits. Everybody lives like that now—nobody works—they " trust their wits." Would you have us

kick the bucket ? Why, we get up off the nests long
before sunrise, search the whole wood up and down—
it's all as bare as your head—not a wild berry, not a
little bird, not a dead beast anywhere. The very worms
have gone and dug themselves deep in the earth.'

The old crow heard all these words and thought deep
thoughts. He remembered some hard times. For
years together starvation pursued the crow tribe : an
untold number of them perished. But in those times
there was a rule : you've got claws—tear your own
breast with them but don't covet another's bit. Yet
even then it was pretty clear that the crow tribe would
not hold out like this for long. To see how others live
on the fat of the land, and starve of your own free will—
this would make any one's heart ache.

And science luckily came to the rescue : peck anything you can and where you can. If you can fill your
crop, fly a free bird, well-fed and happy. If you can't,
hang with a shot through you for a scarecrow in a kitchen
garden ! A la guerre comme à la guerre !

When his old dad brought him, scarcely fledged, to
these parts from beyond three-times-nine far-off seas,
this was a free land—forest and water as far as eye could
reach. In the forest berries of all kinds and beasts and
birds there was a plenty of ; the water swarmed with
fish. Their Head was then as now a hawk, but the hawk
of those days was himself well-fed for one thing, and for
another he was a simple soul—so simple that there are
anecdotes about his simplicity to this day. He did
indeed have a liking for a meal of baby crows, but even

in this he observed justice ; one day he would take a fledgling out of one nest, the next out of another ; and if he saw that the nest was a poor tumble-down one, he would fly off without that even. And the taxation was light in those days : an egg from each nest, a feather from each wing, and a fledgling from every tenth nest as a present to the hawk. If you have done your share you can sleep in peace.

But little by little everything was changed. Man coveted the free places, and began to lay about with his axe. The forests were thinned, the marshes were drained, the river grew shallower. At first on the river bank there appeared settlements, then hamlets, villages, gentlemen's houses. The thud of the axe rang like a dull echo in the very depths of the forest, disturbing the even tenor of the life of birds and beasts. The older members of the crow tribe even then foretold that something sinister threatened, but the young crows circled above the human dwellings with merry cawing, as if in welcome to the new-comers. Their young breasts were tired of the strict teaching of their elders ; they were wearied of the depths of the forest. They wanted something new, unusual, untried. The crow tribe was split into two parties, disputes began, quarrelling, strife. . . .

Simultaneously with this there came a change in the highest ornithological spheres. The old hawk was found to be unequal to his calling. He could govern under a patriarchal system of society, but when relations grew more complex, when at every step new and disturbing elements confronted him in crow life, administrative sagacity deserted him. The heads of the administration called him an old muff; the crow tribe disputed his authority, and shamelessly cawed all sorts of rubbish into his ears, and he instead of nipping the evil in the bud only blinked graciously, and jokingly said, ' Ah, when reform comes in you 'll see what 's what ! ' The expected reform did come in at last. The old hawk was put on the shelf and in his stead was appointed quite a young one. To assist him, as highest controller, they put in a falcon.

The new Heads came and made an ungracious speech to the crow tribe : ' I 'll knock you into a cocked hat ! ' said the hawk, and the falcon added, ' So will I ! ' After that they announced that henceforth the taxes would be trebled, gave out the taxation-forms and flew away.

Then veritable ruin began. The crow tribe raised an outcry : ' They have put on cruel taxes, and given us nothing in return,' was heard all over the forest ; but neither the hawk nor the falcon hearkened to the crows' complaint, and only sent finches to catch the disaffected who perverted the people with vain words. Many nests were ruined then, many of the crow tribe taken into captivity and given to the wolves and to the foxes to eat. They thought that the crows, frightened, would bring tribute on their tails. But the crows only flew hither and thither in panic, cawing : ' Kill us, shoot us, but we have no tribute to give.'

And now it was just the same : the crow tribe was

beggared, but the treasury was not getting filled either. Whatever a crow picked up by the way, the finch took on the way. In fact, things could not be worse. The crow tribe began to think of moving to other parts, and sent scouts to prospect ahead. They set out, but never came back again. Perhaps they got lost, perhaps on the way the finches strangled them, and perhaps they died of starvation. And it's no easy thing, either, to move from your immemorial birthplace to goodness knows where! There are no free places now—man is everywhere. Even he has not room—he goes forward with his axe, the forests groan, the beasts run, and he from morning till night pulls up the tree roots, clears land for the plough, builds log-houses, and at night lies shivering in his earth-hut, cold and hungry, waiting for all this pother to settle into order.

He thought and thought, did the old crow, and at last came to the conclusion that he must go and declare the whole Truth. Only he was old and feeble—could he ever get there? It was no easy matter to make so long a journey. First one must petition the hawk, then the falcon, and lastly the kite who ruled over the crow tribe as a sort of chief official over the district.

Among the birds as among men there are official grades. Everywhere they would ask you, ' Have you been to the hawk? have you been to the falcon? ' and if you haven't, as likely as not you'd be accounted a rebel.

At last, however, he rose from his nest early one morning and flew off. Presently he saw the hawk sitting on a high, high pine-tree. The hawk had fed well that morning and was cleaning his beak with his claws.

' Good-morning, venerable bird,' the hawk greeted him good-humouredly. ' What is your business ? '

' I have come to your worship to declare the truth ! ' cawed the old crow excitedly. ' The crow tribe is perishing . . . perishing. . . . Man destroys them, cruel taxation oppresses them, the finches give them no peace. . . . They are dying and dying, and those that are left have not enough food.'

' Is that so ? And is it not due to their indolence that all these ills have come upon the crow tribe ? '

' You know yourself that indolent we are not. From morning till night we forage, search for food. We live and labour as honest crows should, but to obtain anything by honest means has become impossible.'

The hawk mused a moment as if hesitating to utter the real words, but said at last : ' Use your wits ! '

However, this pronouncement did not satisfy the crow but only agitated him the more.

' I know well enough that nowadays all live by keeping a sharp look-out, but our crow tribe is too simple for that. Others pinch millions and go scot-free, but if a crow steal a halfpenny, it 's death to it. Just think, isn't it a villainy—death for a halfpenny ? And then you say " Use your wits." You have been sent us for a chief, to shield and to protect us, and you do most to ruin us, you oppress us most. How long shall we suffer it ? Why, if we . . .'

The crow broke off in fear. It was not so easy then to declare the Truth !

But the hawk, as has been said already, had fed well that morning, and looked upon his uninvited guest with good humour.

'I know, you need not finish,' he said; 'we've heard this story a long time, but we are still spared, thank God. . . . But you might just make a note of it : you've come here to declare the Truth to me and tripped up at the first word. . . . Have you said all ? '

' All for the moment,' said the crow, still nervous.

' Well, then, I'll tell you this : this Truth of yours every one knows already and has known this long time —not only you crows, but finches and hawks and falcons. Only it does not suit us just now, so however loud you go declaring it—crying it aloud at all the cross-roads— nothing will come of it. And when the time comes, it will declare itself, *when*, no one at present knows. Understand ? '

' This much I understand—that there is an end of the crow tribe, that's all,' the old crow said bitterly.

' You don't understand ? Well, then, let us talk. You say that man destroys you, but can we birds do anything against men ? Man has invented gunpowder, but what can we get against that ? He has invented gunpowder, and fires away at us : does what he pleases to us. We are just like the peasants—we get fired at from every side—the railway, or a new machine, or a bad harvest, or a new tax—all firing at him. The peasants turn and turn that way and this. No one knows how it was that Mr. Jaweasy got road-property, but they have a silver piece the less in their purses—can a poor unlearned man understand that ? But it 's a simple matter. Mr. Jaweasy invented gunpowder, while the peasants, like worms, only knew how to dig in the dung. And if you are a worm, you should live like a worm. Even you crows have no mercy on the worm : think, if he raised an outcry against you, would you not be the first to be astonished ? A crawling worm, and thinks he 'll have a say too ! That 's how it is, my venerable ! The one who gets the better of you is the one who 's right. Now do you understand ? '

' We 've got to perish then ? That 's a cruel word you 've spoken,' said the crow desolately.

' Whether my word is cruel or not is not the point, but the point is, that neither have I kept the Truth from you. Not that Truth which you are seeking, but that which in these times every one must take into account. However, let us continue our talk. You say that the finches rob you of your food as you bring it ; that I, the hawk, rifle your nests ; that instead of being your protectors we do but beggar you. Well, you want to eat and so do we. If you were the stronger, you would eat us ; now we are the stronger—we eat you. That 's truth too. You have declared me your Truth, and I have declared you mine, only my Truth happens here below and yours hovers in the clouds. Understand ? '

' It 's death, it 's death ! ' the old crow kept repeating, scarcely able to gather the meaning of the hawk's

words, but instinctively feeling that they contained
something extraordinarily cruel.

The hawk looked the suppliant over from head to
tail, and as he had fed well, he thought he would have
a joke.

' Shall I just eat you now, eh ? ' he said, but seeing
the crow instinctively jump back, continued : ' There
now ! as if I would—you 're too old and bony. Undo
your waistcoat a minute.'

The crow spread his wings and was himself surprised : skin and bone he was—no down, no feathers
—even a hungry wolf wouldn't look at a bird like
that.

' Just see what you are like now. And all because
you will keep thinking about the Truth. If only you
lived like a proper crow, without thinking, you wouldn't
be like that. But there, it 's time we had done ! You
complain too that cruel taxes are laid on you—and that
is true. But think—whom else is there to take it off ?
Sparrows, tits, siskins, chaffinches ? It 's not much any
of them can give. Woodcock, blackcock, bustards,
woodpeckers, cuckoos—these all live by themselves,
you can't find them with a candle by daylight as the
saying goes. Only the crows live in a community,
like regular peasants, and moreover perpetually announce their presence—well, what wonder that they
get on the census ? And once on the census—look
out, of course ! And if of late years the taxes have
been heavier, that 's because there is greater need.
Greater need—greater taxation. So that 's how it is,

my venerable. You 've told the Truth and I 've told the Truth, and whose Truth is the stronger your crows' existence proves. Now get along home, for I want a bit of a sleep.'

However, the old crow did not go home, but directed his flight to the falcon.

' Come what may,' thought he, heavily flapping his old wings, ' I 'll carry the thing through to the end. If the falcon won't take my Truth I 'll go to the goubernia, to the kite himself, but I will not abandon the pursuit of justice.'

The falcon lived in a mountain ravine, and access to him was very difficult. At the entrance to his dwelling a finch always sat on duty, receiving petitioners. At this moment it happened to be Iván Ivánovitch, well known to all the crow tribe. He was the falcon's favourite (report said even that he was the falcon's illegitimate son), trusted with the most important and secret affairs. This was a darc-devil fellow, in appearance good-natured, with nice and even refined manners. He was not averse to a little chat and a joke, to going on the spree a bit, behind a cloud, to flying at catch-who-catch-can now and again with the girls, the linnets, and even to doing a good turn to a friend—but all this good nature was his only while he was not on duty. As soon as he was at his official post (especially on confidential missions) he was instantly another creature. He became cold, severe, and efficient to the point of cruelty. If he had orders to catch any one, he would catch him ; if he had orders to strangle any one, he would strangle

him.   If a bird was twice as big and strong as he, he
would come at it with such force that it would begin to
yell and rush about before he got to it.   Indeed, the
birds whom he had ever dealt with would quake with
fear at his very name.

' Still dreaming, old fellow ? ' Iván Ivánovitch greeted
the petitioner.

The old crow understood that here everything was
already known.   Birds have their secret service through
which not only the populace's actions but their inmost
thoughts are known to them.

' The old haven't much chance of dreaming,' he said
evasively.

' Come to declare the Truth, eh ?   However, that 's
your own business.   Shall I announce you ? '

' If you would be so kind.'

Iván Ivánovitch dived into the ravine and was away
there about an hour.   The crow waited for his return
with quaking heart.   At last he reappeared.

' I am to tell you,' he announced, ' that the Head
hasn't time to have a chat with you.   This Truth of yours
is known to every one, it has a flaw in it anyway, since
of its own self it does not come to light.   You 've a rest-
less character, and talk vain, dangerous talk to the
people.   You should for this have long ago been eaten,
only you 're so old and thin and feeble.   Going to the
Head of the district, I suppose, now ? '

' N-no . . . what 's the good . . .? ' the crow tried to get
out of it.

' Don't prevaricate.   I see through you !   Well, go

on then, only take care they don't peck your eyes
out for this Truth of yours. Don't make a mess
of it now ! You don't even know the way, I suppose ?
Here—see that cloud ? It's just there—above that
cloud.'

Despite the finch's prediction, the crow decided to
carry his petition through. By a long and circuitous
way he mounted, spending the night in animals'
abandoned lairs, feeding on berries he occasionally
found on the mountain spurs. At length he cut into
the cloud, and before his eyes a wondrous spectacle
appeared.

Several mountain summits, massed close together,
snow-covered, burned in the rays of the rising sun.
From afar it seemed like a fairy castle at whose foot
clouds lay immovable, and above, for a roof, stretched
endlessly the deep blue of the sky.

The kite sat on a crag, surrounded by a whole crowd
of various kinds of birds. On his right hand sat a white
falcon, his assistant and councillor ; at his feet tumbled
all sorts of secretaries on special commissions, parrots,
learned bullfinches, and siskins ; from the back a chorus
of starlings read out the morning's post ; close by, on a
separate summit, dozed owls of various kinds, and bats,
forming an official council ; numbers of crows flitted
hither and thither with quills behind their ears, writing
out orders, instructions, and documents, and shouting
' Caw, caw, all hot, all hot, caw, caw, five kopeks the
lot ! '

The kite was **very very old**, and scarcely able to rattle

his beak from age. At the moment when the crow descended at his feet he had just dined, and in a comatose condition, with closed eyes, sat with nodding head, in spite of the deafening talk and noise.

However, the petitioner's arrival made a good deal of stir among the birds, which caused the kite to wake up.

' Come with a little request, venerable bird ? ' he asked the crow kindly.

' I have come from far-off lands, your Excellency,' the crow began with exaltation, ' to declare the Truth to you,' but was at once stopped by the falcon.

' Don't go in for rhetoric,' he said coldly, ' state your business without digression, concisely and simply, point by point. What do you want ? '

The crow began to detail his petition point by point : man destroys the crow tribe ; finches, hawks, falcons worry it ; cruel taxation ruins it. . . .

And every time he made a point, the kite creakingly opened his beak and pronounced : ' You are right, venerable bird.'

The old crow's heart burned within him at this assent. ' At last,' he thought, ' I shall see this " Truth " which I have thirsted for since I was young ! I will serve my tribe, I will strive for it ! ' And the longer his speech went on, the more and more inspired he became. At last he spoke out all he had in his heart and stopped.

' Have you said everything ? ' the kite asked him.

' Everything,' the crow answered.

' You have been to the hawk and to the falcon with your petition ? '

' I have.' He briefly told the kite of his conversation with the hawk and of his unsuccessful visit to the falcon.

' Then this is what I will tell you of this Truth of yours. More than two hundred years I have sat upon this cliff and at least sideways have looked at the sun—but at any rate I have looked. But not once have I been able to look in the face of Truth.'

' But why ? ' wonderingly cawed the crow.

' Because a bird cannot grasp it—has not the strength. If any one thinks he has grasped the Truth, he must obey it, and we cannot obey it, that is why we can never afford to look it full in the face. We keep thinking, "Maybe it will go past and not trouble us."' A moment the kite sat lost in reverie, and then went on : ' It is a cruel word the hawk spoke to you, but he is right. Truth is good, but not at all times and not in all places is it meet to listen to it. Some it may lead into temptation, to some it may seem a reproach. Some would be glad to serve Truth, but how are they to meet it with empty hands ? Truth is not a crow : you cannot catch it by the tail. Look round you : everywhere there is strife, everywhere quarrelling, no one can rightly tell why and where he is going. . . . That is why each talks of *his* own particular truth. But the time will come when every breathing thing will clearly see the rightful limits within which his life must run its course. Then of itself the strife will end, and with it disappear like smoke the little " personal truths." One real and all-compelling Truth will manifest itself; it will come, and the world will shine in radiance. And we shall live in harmony and love. That 's how it is, ancient one ! And in the meantime go home in peace, and tell the crow tribe that I put my trust in them as in a rock.'

THE FOOL

In the days of long ago—in the time of King Peascod it was—a pair of clever parents had a son who was a fool. When he was still an infant they used to wonder whom Ivànoushka took after. Mamma used to say it was after papa, and papa after mamma, and at last after some thought they came to the conclusion that it was after both.

It was not that they had a fool for a son that disconcerted the parents—a fool—and especially if sent to Court—why you couldn't wish for better—but it was that he was a special kind of fool, for whom, if one didn't look out, one would likely have to answer to the Authorities. He would go and do a lot of fool things, go and make a mess of things, and by what right—under what law ?

There are light kinds of fools, but this one there was no understanding. Now Militrissa Kirbityevna, who lived close by, had a son Lëvka—a fool too. He would run out barefoot into the street, let his sleeves down and hop about on one foot, shouting at the top of his voice, ' Tweet, tweet, Lëvka's beat, beat, beat, bom, boom.' They would catch him at once, and put him in the lock-up—just sit there a bit ! He was even shown to the Governor when he came for an inspection and he commended him. ' Take care of him. We need fools.'

But *this* fool was an extraordinary one. He would be

211

sitting at home, reading a book or kissing his mother or his father and being petted, when suddenly—nothing to account for it—his heart would be as on fire. He would run off, the earth just quaking under him. If anything needed to be approached gradually, indirectly, he would dash straight bang in; if any word should be forgotten altogether, he would come out with it slap. It made you laugh and cry. You could shout at him, you could beat him, he felt nothing, heard nothing. He would just do what he had a mind to, and run home to mammy and daddy.

' What is the matter, my precious one ? Sit down and rest, my darling ! '

' I am not tired, mammy.'

' Where have you been, my dearie ? You run off and never tell any one.'

' I 've been to Lëvka's, mammy darling. Lëvka is ill and he asked me for a bun. I took a bun off the counter at the baker's and brought it him.'

His mother, hearing these words, would be aghast.

' Oh, you 'll kill me, oh you 'll be the death of me ! What *have* you done ? You 've stolen a bun ! '

' How stolen it ? What 's " stolen " ? '

Ever so many times the neighbours warned mamma and papa.

' Can't you stop your fool ? He will cause you dreadful trouble one of these days ! '

But the parents could do nothing. They only thought : ' It 's easy to say " Can't you stop him ? " How are you to stop him ? How can people not under-

stand that a parent's heart is torn more for a fool of a
son than for a wise one ? '

And papa would begin to reason with the fool : ' A
bun is private property ! ' And it would seem as if he
understood : ' Yes, papa darling ? ' But if Lëvka
appeared at that moment—' Give me a bun, Vanya ! '
—off he would bolt, and sure enough pinch a bun off the
counter ! There was no understanding whether he had
stolen it or not !

The baker stood it for some time, but at last he took
the huff : he sent to the police station. The policeman
came to the parents and said, ' I am very sorry, madam,
but you 'll have to whip your fool.'

The parents' hearts bled—but there was nothing for
it. Papa saw that the policeman was right : he whipped
the fool. But the fool did not understand in the least.
When he felt that it hurt, he cried a little, but did not
call out ' What is it for ? ' nor ' I won't do it again ! '
Rather he seemed to be surprised that his father should
wish to do such a thing.

So the lesson was lost on Ivànoushka : just as he had
been a fool before the whipping, so a fool he remained
after it. He would see Lëvka from the window, hop-
ping barefoot in the street, and run out to him, take off
his boots, let down his sleeves and his shirt, and begin
to do what Lëvka did.

' What a thing to do ! ' his mother would say angrily.
' Tease a poor fool ! '

' I am not teasing him, mammy darling. I am playing with him, because it 's dull for him all by himself.'

' Go on twirling, go on, and you 'll turn into a fool yourself ! '

And papa, hearing this conversation, would break in :

' He should be whipped, and she talks to him ! Talk a little more and there 'll be something to see. If you had lifted his shirt oftener he would have been a proper boy before now.'

And all the neighbours commended papa : for one thing because there was a law that fools should be taught, and for another, there was no peace for any one from Ivànoushka now.

One day some neighbouring boys set to teasing a goat—he began to defend the goat. He stood in front of him and would not let them hurt him. The goat butted him from behind, the boys trounced him from in front, and he never turned a hair : they brought him home black and blue ! And the next day another affair : he took a cockerel away from the cook. The cook was carrying a cockerel under his arm to the kitchen.

' Where are you taking the cockerel to, Kouzmà ? ' says the fool.

' Why, to the kitchen of course and into the soup ! . . .'

The fool fell upon him, and before the cook could turn round, there was the cock sitting on the fence, flapping his wings.

Papa explained and explained to him : ' The cock is not yours, you are not to take it away from the cook.' And he in answer just said the same thing over and over again : ' I know he 's not mine, but he isn't the cook's either—he is his own.'

214

Although all the household loved the fool for his quiet and affectionate ways, in the course of time he managed to plague them all with what he did. If he was hungry he would never ask his mother properly, ' Please, mamma dear, may I take a tart from the sideboard ? ' —he would go and turn everything upside down in the cupboard or the kitchen, and whatever he found he would just eat, without so much as by your leave. If he had a mind to go out he would take his cap, and just go without asking. Once a beggar stopped outside mamma's window, and it so chanced a three-rouble note lay on the table. He took it and put it into the beggar's bag.

' Goodness ! He 'll be a regular Cartouche,' wailed his mother.

' Of course he will,' his father said, ' and worse too, if you are going to la-de-da like this with him instead of whipping him. You go havering on with him.'

There was nothing to be done, mamma too whipped the fool. But she whipped him, to tell the truth, only a very little, only just for a lesson. And he, the blessed creature, got up, his face all tear-stained, and put his arms round his mother's neck, ' Oh mammy, mammy. My poor, poor darling mammy ! '

And suddenly mamma was so ashamed that she began to cry too.

' My blessed, darling little fool ! If only the Lord would take both of us ! '

At last, however, he nearly did for his mother and for himself. They were all taking a walk along the river bank. Mamma and papa were walking arm-in-arm and he was in front, playing at being a scout—that they were discovering the source of the Niger and he was sent on to see if there were any danger ahead. Suddenly he heard a moaning : they looked at the river and there was somebody's little boy struggling in the water. They had not time to turn round before the fool was slap in the river, and after the fool mamma, just as she was, in her crinoline, found herself in the water. And after mamma a couple of policemen in uniform. And papa stood on the bank, flapping his arms like wings : ' Mine, save mine ! ' At last the policemen pulled out all the three of them. Mamma got off with a fright, but the fool lay a month in bed with a fever.

Whether he understood that he had acted like a fool, or whether he was sorry for his mother when he came to and saw her, thin and pale, sitting at his bedside, he burst into tears. He kept saying over and over again, ' Mammy, mammy darling, why *didn't* God take us ? '

And papa was standing there too, and hoped that at any rate now the fool would say, ' Forgive me, papa dear, and I won't do it any more ! ' But he didn't.

After this papa and mamma had a serious talk as to what was to be done with the fool. They walked up and down the drawing-room, with their arms round each other, discussing the problem from every point of view, and for a long time could not agree upon a course of action.

The thing was that papa was a just man. At home, abroad, and out in the street he always insisted upon the same thing : ' Wherefore make laws if you do not observe them ? ' His very appearance suggested it amusingly—as if he were holding a pair of scales in one hand and just going to drop half an ounce of retribution in with the other. Hence, and taking into consideration all the aforementioned occurrences, he required that Ivànoushka should be treated with all the rigour of the domestic law.

' He has transgressed, therefore he must bear a corresponding punishment. Look.'

And he showed mamma a little table on which was displayed :

Name of the transgressor.	Number of blows with switch.	
	From	To
Departure from rules of subordination.	5	7

But mamma was mamma—and nothing more. She did not deny justice, but understood it in some primitive sense, as the common people do when they speak of a ' just man.' No punishment, but as a kind of dispensation. And little versed as she was in matters of jurisprudence, once she put papa to shame :

' What are we going to punish him for ? ' she said. ' For wanting to save a drowning child ? Think ! '

Nevertheless, papa insisted that the fool could no longer be kept at home but must be sent to an institution.

The quiet regularity of the institution life had at first a beneficial effect on the fool. Nothing stimulated his impressionable nature nor roused in him the sudden activity of the soul. In the first years he did not even learn, but simply assimilated the material for learning. Nor were there any acute differences in the states of his fellow-pupils which called out the need to comfort, to help. Success in learning was dependent chiefly on memory, and as Ivànoushka had an excellent memory and moreover the kindest of dispositions, he was very nearly transformed from a fool into a clever boy.

' What did I tell you ? ' said papa triumphantly.

' Well, well, don't be cross,' mamma answered, as if apologising for having been in a hurry to shame papa.

But as the complexity of the curriculum increased, Ivànoushka's life became more difficult. The majority of subjects he could not understand at all. He could not understand History, Jurisprudence, nor the Science of the Accumulation and the Distribution of Wealth. Not that he did not want to understand, but he simply could not, and to all the teachings of his preceptors answered always one and the same thing : ' That cannot be so ! '

Once more papa was disconcerted and began to reproach mamma that Ivànoushka took after her. But mamma no longer listened to his reproaches, and only cried all day without stopping. Was it possible that Ivànoushka would remain a fool all his days ?

' Won't you at any rate *pretend* that you understand ? ' she entreated Ivànoushka. ' Force yourself to understand a little—there, let me show you.'

She would open the book and read :

' On the rules of inheritance under the law for those connected by the bond of common maternity,' and could not understand a thing ! And they would both cry, the fool and his mother.

And papa meanwhile was reeling it off like a book :

' Those connected by the bond of common maternity must be distinguished in the first place from those connected by common parentage, in the second place from those who having common maternity have likewise common parentage, and thirdly from . . .'

' There, how well papa knows it ! ' mamma would say wonderingly, as she shed bitter tears.

Seeing his mother cry, the fool would pull himself together and make an immense effort. He would go and sit in a corner at recreation time, and take a book, put his fingers in his ears, and learn it by heart. So well he would learn it, so well he would say it in class. . . . And suddenly he would come out with something about Alexander of Macedon so appalling that the teacher's three remaining hairs would stand upright on his bald head.

' Sit down,' the teacher would say ' A saddening fate awaits you in the future ! Never will you become a statesman. Thank God He has given you parents who have never been under suspicion. If it had not been for that . . . Sit down, and try not to wound your preceptors by disgraceful exhibitions ! '

And it was so : it was only in view of his parents' good behaviour that the fool was moved up from class to class and eventually given a certificate when he left the institution. But when he brought the certificate home, mamma looked at it and straightway burst into tears. And papa asked sternly :

' What have you been doing, you feelingless dolt ? '

' I was just . . . I expect it 's a sort of rule in the institution, papa. . . .'

He did not even stop to explain properly : saw Lëvka in the street and ran off.

Lëvka he was fonder of than ever, because the poor fool was now even more pitiable. He was just as thin and went about barefoot as he did six years ago, and held his hands with his fingers all spread, but his face was overgrown with hair now and he was lank as a lamp-post. Militrissa Kirbityevna had disowned him long ago : she no longer fed him and scarcely dressed him even. So he was always hungry, and if it had not been for the tender-hearted woman who sold buns he would have died of hunger ! But most of all he suffered from the street boys. They gave him no rest : they teased him, they set dogs on him, they pinched his legs, they pulled his shirt. The whole day long you heard his howls, accompanied by the idiotic clanking of his teeth. He howled from the pain, but did not understand where it came from.

The fool protected Lëvka, took him in to get warm, fed him and clothed him. All that Lëvka needed, Ivànoushka took without asking, or if he did not know where to find it, he demanded it in a tone that clearly showed the very notion of refusal never occurred to him.

Only fools have such conviction in their tone, such directness in their gaze. He was afraid of no one and of nothing, felt a disgust of nothing, and had no idea of danger. Seeing the Ispravnik,[1] he did not run to the other side of the street, but walked straight on as if he had been guilty of nothing. If there was a fire in the town, he was the first to go into it : if he heard there was any one seriously ill, he used to run in, sit down at the bedside and help to look after the invalid. He even found wise words at these times, as if he had not been a fool at all. Only one thing lay like a stone on his heart : his mother spent sleepless nights while he played his fool tricks. But there was something inevitable as destiny, something which fatally led him to self-abasement and self-sacrifice, and he obeyed that impulse instinctively, regardless of obvious consequences, and allowing no compromise even in favour of blood ties.

Many times his parents thought of what they could put the fool to to make him a little bit more like an ordinary human. Papa appointed him once to a post of a sort of patron of the local school (without a salary even a fool will do, and with one he will for sure!), but the fool immediately raised such a to-do there, that only in consideration of the excellent reputation of his parents did the Ispravnik agree to hush the matter up. Then mamma hit on the plan of marrying the fool ! Perhaps God would loose his bonds. They found him a suitable bride—a young widow from the trading class—Mrs.

[1] Captain of the district police.—*Tr.*

Podvòhina. She was a very good-looking young woman and had two shops in the market-square. She lived virtuously in her widowhood, her wares were always of the best quality, and she managed her trade with ability and independence. In fact, one could not have made a better match. She took a fancy to the fool too. His appearance was presentable, his behaviour mild. She even would not allow, like others, that he was deficient in mind, but held that his mind needed to be set free, and had full confidence of achieving success in this.

But all the fool's instincts were so completely un-awakened that even that kindly and modest woman was astonished. Not once did he start at her touch, not once did he show any confusion, or feel any of that embarrassment to which women display such heartfelt sympathy, instinctively detecting in them the first, the sweetest tremors of love. The fool would come, eat his dinner, drink his tea, and evidently not understand in the slightest why he was at Mrs. Podvòhina's instead of at home.

'How is it you don't get weary of things? You understand nothing,' the beautiful widow would say.

'Oh yes, I *am* very weary of things! They say it is because I have no occupation.'

'Then find an occupation. . . . Love some one.'

'But, dear me, how is it possible not to love people? One must love everybody : the happy people because they have managed to make themselves happy, the unhappy ones because they have no joys.'

And so this marriage never came off.

The widow Podvòhina grieved a little, and even promised to wait for a year, but after holding out for a month or two, got married at Christmas to the mayor, Lihodèyev. Now they have four shops in the market-square : on weekdays they trade in all the four—she in the drapery line, he in wines and spirits : and on Sundays they entertain the Ispravnik and others of the Authorities on meat pies.

But the fool just lived at home unconcerned.

' If only God would put him out of the way,' papa used to whisper low so that mamma could not hear.

Mamma prayed continually and put her trust in God's grace. Might the Lord enlighten Ivànoushka's mind with understanding, lead his steps in the way of his honour the Ispravnik, of his Assistant, and of the Members of the Board. Surely he must get some kind of post ! It was impossible that there was something for every one to do, but nothing for him alone.

Only one man looked at him with other eyes, and he was only a chance visitor. He was passing the town and turned in to see papa, because he was a very old friend of his. They talked and talked, they remembered old times, they recalled the follies of their youth, and by the way they touched upon the present too. Papa shut the door, just in case, and they told each other all about everything.

They didn't say it, but each thought to himself, ' So that 's what sort of a fellow you are, old man ! ' Naturally papa complained about his fool too, and as no one now troubled to spare his feelings, they just called him ' the fool ' in his presence. The guest was interested by the tales about the fool, stopped the night with his friend, and the next day he said :

' He isn't a fool at all. It 's only that he has no depraved thoughts—and so he cannot accommodate himself. There are others who gradually rid themselves of depraved thoughts, but this process costs them enormous effort, and often results in a grave moral crisis. But he has had no need of such effort because he has not got the kind of pores in his organism through which a depraved thought could creep in. Nature herself has given him this. However, undoubtedly there will come a moment when the tide of life will by its tyrannical strength force him to choose between being a fool and depravity. Then he will *understand*. Only I should not advise you to hurry on that moment, because as soon as it arrives there will not be a more unhappy creature in this world. And then—I am convinced of it—he will prefer to remain a fool.'

The guest said his say and went on from the town. And papa set to work thinking. He went over all his life, remembering what depraved thoughts he had had and in what manner he had freed himself from them. And of course, sternly though he examined himself, he came out with honour. Never had he had any base thoughts and consequently had felt no need of freeing himself from them. Why, then, was he not a fool ?

At last he came to the conclusion that his old friend had fuddled his brains. . . . ' There they live in their Petersburg dens, cultivating themselves. They cultivate and cultivate till they can talk in nothing but lies. And we here in Poshekhónie, we don't cultivate ourselves, but we don't lie—that's safer. It's all lies : there's no gift of Nature in being a fool, and if by the grace of God my fool will some day become wise, he will certainly not be made miserable by it, but will get a post and live happily like the rest of us.'

Having settled this he waited : from day to day he expected Ivànoushka suddenly to shine forth and to be given an important appointment. But instead, one fine day, they told him that the fool had disappeared from home.

.   .   .   .

Years passed. The old parents nearly cried their eyes out. They did not for one moment stop expecting him. They had not one thought which directly or indirectly did not relate to him. The old couple lost all memory except of one thing : Where was he now ? Was he fed ? Was he clothed ? A very little will kill a fool. I would not wish an enemy the experience of that torture of a parent's heart, which blames itself .for everything, which is torn by every childish moan echoing a thousand times.

However, the fool did return. But of the formerly radiantly healthy fool there was not left a trace. He was white, emaciated, exhausted. Where had he been

wandering ?   What had he seen ?   Had he understood,
or not ?   Nobody could get anything out of him.   He
came home and spoke no more.

In any case, the passing guest had been right : to the
day of his death he was always called a *fool*.

THE WILD SQUIRE

I N a certain kingdom, in a certain country, once upon a
time there lived a squire—he lived, and rejoiced. He
had a plenty of everything, peasants, and corn, and
cattle, and land, and orchards. And he was stupid, this
squire, he read the newspaper *Vyest*,[1] and his flesh was
soft, white, and plump.

And once this squire prayed aloud to God :

' Oh Lord ! I am thankful to Thee for everything, I
have my reward in everything ! Only one thing my
heart turns against—there are such a lot of peasants
in our land ! '

But God knew that the squire was a stupid man, and
hearkened not to his prayer.

The squire saw that there were no fewer peasants, but
every day more—he saw it and was filled with fear :
' And what if the peasant eats up all my substance ? '

The squire would look at the paper *Vyest*, to see what
one should do in such a case, and there would read,
' Make efforts ! '

' So few words,' the stupid squire would say, ' but
what precious words ! '

And he would begin making efforts—and not just
anyhow, but all according to rule. If a peasant's
chicken strayed into the squire's oats, it was straightway popped—according to rule—into the soup ; if a
peasant chopped some wood from the squire's forest on

---

[1] News.—*Tr.*

227

the quiet—immediately the wood was hauled off to
the squire's yard and the peasant, according to rule,
fined.

' I get a greater effect on them by these fines,' the
squire said to his neighbours, ' because they understand
it, you see.'

The peasants saw that though theirs was a stupid
squire, yet he was endowed with great sense. He got
them so that they could not so much as pop their noses
out ; wherever you look it 's all ' Not Allowed,' ' Forbidden,' and ' Not yours.' If the cattle went out to
drink, the squire called out, ' It 's *my* water ! ' If a hen
strayed out beyond the fence, the squire called out,
' It 's *my* land ! ' The land and the water and the air—
it had all become his ! The peasant hadn't as much as a
chip of wood to light, a twig to sweep his hut with.
And the peasants prayed to the Lord, the whole
village of them :

' Oh Lord, it is better for us and our children to perish,
than to suffer like this all our lives.'

Merciful God heard the orphans' prayer rising from
every part of the stupid squire's domain. Where the
peasants went to, no one noticed ; men only saw how,
suddenly in a hurricane, a cloud of chaff arose, and like a
blackness in the air, a cloud of peasants' homespun
breeks whisked by. The squire came out on the
verandah, smelt the air, and lo, it was clean and pleasant
in all his domain. Naturally, he was pleased. He
thought, ' Now shall I indulge my flesh—my white,
soft, plump flesh ! '

And he began to live as he liked, and thought of how he could amuse himself.

'I will have,' he thought, 'a theatre here! I will write to the actor Sadovsky, "Come along here, my friend, and bring some actresses with you."'

The actor Sadovsky consented, he came himself and brought actresses with him. But directly he arrived, he saw that the squire's house was empty—there was not a soul to arrange the theatre, no one to work the curtain.

'What on earth have you done with your peasants?' Sadovsky asked.

'Ah that?—oh, God in answer to my prayer has cleared the peasants off all my estate.'

'Good Lord, you *are* a stupid squire! Who brings you water to wash with?'

'Oh, I've gone unwashed for several days now.'

'Want to grow mushrooms on your face, I suppose?' said Sadovsky, and with that took himself off, and all the actresses with him.

The squire called to mind that there were four generals he knew living near by, and he said, 'Why do I keep on laying out Patience all day? I'll try my hand at a game of five!'

No sooner said than done. He wrote the invitations, fixed the day, and sent off the letters.

The generals were real ones, but hungry, and therefore came immediately. They came and marvelled greatly how clean and pleasant the air had become.

'Ah, that,' boasted the squire, 'is because God in

answer to my prayer has cleared the peasants off my land.'

' Oh, how nice that is ! ' said the generals approvingly ; ' then you won't have any of that common people's smell now ? '

' Not a whiff,' said the squire.

They had a game of cards and then another. The generals began to feel it was the time for their drink of vodka. They looked about them uneasily.

' I expect you would like some refreshment, generals,' the squire asked.

' It would be pleasant, my dear sir ! '

He got up, went to the cupboard and took out an acid drop and a gingerbread apiece.

' What is this ? ' asked the generals, with their eyes starting out of their heads.

' There, have something to eat—what I can offer you.'

' If you don't mind, we should so like a little meat !— just a little meat, you know.'

' Well, do you know, I haven't any meat, generals, because since God has delivered me from the peasant, the stove in the kitchen has not been lit.'

The generals were very angry. Even their teeth began to rattle.

' But you must fill your belly with something your-self,' they fell upon him.

' I have raw stuff of sorts, and then there are the gingerbreads still. . . .'

' Well, you *are* a fool of a squire,' said the generals, and leaving their game unfinished, trailed off to their homes.

The squire noticed that he had been called a fool for the second time, and was just about to fall a-thinking, when his eye caught the pack of cards—and leaving everything he began to lay out Patience.

'We 'll see, Mr. Liberals,' he said, ' who 'll get the better of this—I 'll prove to you what true firmness of character can do.'

He was laying out ' The Ladies' Whim,' and thought, ' If it comes out three times, it means I must not give in.' And it just kept coming out over and over again. He had no possible doubt.

' Well, if fortune herself directs me, I must be firm to the end. But meanwhile I have had enough of Patience. I will go and occupy myself for a time.'

And he would walk about the rooms a little, and then would sit down a bit. And all the time he would be thinking. He would think of what machines he would get from England, to get everything done by steam, so as not to have the smell of the common people at all. He would think of the orchard he would make—the pears, the plums, and here and there would be peaches, and here a walnut-tree ! He would look out of the window, and there it would all be—trees, loaded with fruit ! He would think of the cows he would breed, such cows that there would be no skin or flesh—nothing but milk—just all milk ; of what strawberries he would put in—double strawberries, three berries to the pound, and of how much he would sell it for in Moscow. And in his sleep, his dreams were even more amusing than his day-dreams. He dreamt, for instance, that the

Governor himself had heard of this firmness of his and asked the Ispravnik, ' What is this strong-minded son of a hen you 've got in your parts ? ' Then he dreamt that for this same strong-mindedness he was made a Minister and went about with ribbons, and wrote circulars : ' An order to be firm and not to deviate.' Then he dreamt he was walking about on the shores of the Euphrates and Tigris. . . . 'Eve, my love,' he said . . .

But now he had gone through all his dreams : it was time to get up.

' Senka ! ' he called out forgetfully—but suddenly remembered and hung his head.

' Now, what could I occupy myself with however ? Wish to goodness fate would bring me some devil or other.'

And just as he had said this, who should arrive but the Captain Ispravnik himself ! The stupid squire was inordinately glad to see him ; he ran to the cupboard, took out two gingerbreads, and thought to himself, ' Well, this man will be pleased for sure.'

' Tell me, sir, how is it that your serfs have apparently all disappeared ? ' the Ispravnik asked.

' Well, you see, in answer to my prayer God has cleared my land of the peasant completely.'

' I see . . . yes. . . . And I suppose you can tell me, sir, who will pay taxes for them ? '

' Taxes ? Why they !—they themselves, that is their most sacred duty and obligation.'

' I see . . . yes. . . . And how do you suppose these taxes can be got from them when they, in answer to your prayer, are scattered over the face of the earth ? '

' Ah, that . . . well, really, I don't know. . . . *I* will not consent to pay them.'

' And are you aware, sir, that the Treasury cannot exist without taxes and imposts, not to speak of the wine and salt duties ? '

' Why, as to that . . . I am ready . . . a glass of vodka. . . . I will contribute that.'

' But do you know that, owing to your action, in our market one cannot get a piece of meat or a pound of bread ?   Are you aware what this smacks of ? '

' Dear me, but I assure you I should be most glad to send in something.   Here are two whole gingerbreads ! '

' You 're an awful fool, sir,' said the Ispravnik, turned, and went off without so much as looking at the gingerbreads.

This time the squire fell to thinking seriously.   Here was the third person calling him a fool, the third person who looked at him, spat, and went off.   Could he really be a fool ?   This firmness which he so cherished in his heart, was it only foolishness and madness ?   And could it be that solely in consequence of his firmness the taxes and imposts had stopped, and one could not get a pound of flour or a piece of meat in the market ?

And, as he was a fool of a squire, at first he burst out laughing at the pleasure of the thought, what a trick he had played, but then he remembered the Ispravnik's words : ' Are you aware what this smacks of ? ' and fell into a considerable funk.   He walked up and down the rooms, as was his custom, and kept thinking, ' What does it smack of ? does it smack of imprisonment . . . ? or exile . . . ? '

' If it is exile, at any rate the world would be convinced of my firmness,' said the squire, and to himself he thought, ' In exile, perhaps, I would see my good old peasants.' He would walk about, and sit a little, and walk about again.

Whatever he went up to, it all seemed to say to him, ' You 're an awful fool, sir ! ' Suddenly he saw a young mouse running across the room and stealing softly towards the cards with which he played Patience and which he had made greasy enough to whet a mouse's appetite.

' Ksh ! ' he fell on the mouse.

But he was a clever young mouse, and understood that the squire could do him no harm without Senka. It only whisked its tail in answer to the squire's terrifying voice, and in a moment was looking out at him from under the sofa, as if saying, ' Wait, you stupid squire, this is nothing. I shall not only eat your cards, but your dressing-gown too, when it 's greasy enough ! '

No one knows how long after this was, but one fine day the squire noticed that his garden paths were overgrown with thistles, that in the bushes snakes and pests of all kinds swarmed, and in the park wild beasts howled. Once a bear came up to the very house, sat down on his haunches, looking in through the window at the squire, and licked his chops.

' Senka ! ' called out the squire, but suddenly remembered—and began to cry.

Nevertheless his firmness of purpose never left him. Several times he was just weakening, but as soon as he felt that his heart was beginning to give way, he immediately rushed to the newspaper, *Vyest*, and in one moment he was adamant again.

' No, I 'd rather grow quite a savage, I 'd rather wander with the wild beasts in the forests, than that any one should say that a Russian nobleman, Prince Ouroussov-Koutchoum-Kildibaev, went back on his principles ! '

And so he grew into a savage. Although by that time autumn had already set in, and there were considerable frosts, he did not even feel the cold. He grew hair all over, like Esau, and his nails got hard as iron. He had long left off wiping his nose, he went about mostly on all fours, and even wondered how he had not noticed before that this method of locomotion was the most respectable and the easiest. He even lost the ability of pronouncing articulate sounds, and got a kind of special cry of victory—intermediate between a whistle, hiss, and roar. But he had not as yet grown a tail.

He would go out into his park, where he used to pamper his white, soft, plump body, run up a tree in a twinkling, like a cat, and watch. A hare would come along, sit up on its hind legs and listen—if there were danger from anywhere—and he would be on the watch. Like a dart he would leap from the trees, seize his prey, tear it up with his nails, and eat it, with the entrails and the skin even.

And he got tremendously strong, so strong, he considered he had a right to be friends with the bear that used to look at him through the window.

'Ivan Mikhaelych,' he said to the bear, 'shall we make raids on the hares together ? '

'Well, I don't mind if we do,' the bear answered. 'Only, my dear fellow, it's a pity you destroyed that peasant ! '

'How's that ? '

'Why, because it was a deal handier to eat, that peasant, than you noblemen ! And so I'll tell you straight : you are a fool of a squire, though, my friend ! '

Meanwhile the Captain Ispravnik, although he was friendly to the squire, in view of such a fact as the disappearance of the peasant from the land, did not dare to overlook it.

The Government Authorities were perturbed by his report, and wrote : ' And who do you think will pay the taxes ? Who will drink wine in the public-houses ? Who will occupy themselves with innocent pursuits ? ' The Captain Ispravnik answered : ' The Treasury will now have to be abolished, and the innocent pursuits have been abolished of themselves, and instead of them there have sprung up robberies and murders and violence. A few days ago he, the Ispravnik, was nearly killed by some creature—neither a bear nor a man, and this man-bear is suspected of being the said fool of a squire, who was the cause of all this disorder.'

The Authorities were perturbed and called a council. They passed a resolution that the peasant should be caught and established, and it should be intimated to the stupid squire, who had caused all this disturbance, in the most delicate way possible, that he should stop his fallals.

As luck would have it, just at that time a swarm of peasants was flying over the country town, and covered the whole market-square. At once they cleared the creatures off, put them in a basket, and sent them to the district.

And suddenly in the district arose again the smell of chaff, bread, and sheepskin ; but at the same time in the market appeared flour and meat and all sorts of live-stock, and so much was collected in duties that the Treasurer, seeing such a heap of money, just raised his hands and cried, ' Wherever do you get it from, you beggars ? '

What became of the squire ? my readers will ask me.—Well, though with much difficulty, he was caught. Having caught him, they wiped his nose, washed him, and cut his nails. Then the Captain Ispravnik made him a suitable admonition, took away the newspaper *Vyest*, and consigning him to Senka's supervision, went off.

The squire is living to this day. He lays out Patience, misses his former life in the woods, washes only under compulsion, and from time to time gives vent to mooing.

CHRIST'S NIGHT

(*Traditional Tale*)

THE plain still lay in torpor, but in the deep silence of the night from under the snow covering came the voice of the awakening brooks. In the gulleys and hollows these voices rose to a dull roar, warning the traveller of the pitfalls under these places in the road mined with rivulets. But the forest was still silent beneath its weight of hoar-frost, like a ballad-hero in his iron helmet. The dark sky was covered thick with stars, shedding upon the earth a cold and tremulous light. By their deceptive glimmer the villages showed like black patches, sunk in the snowdrift. A desolate, abandoned, wretched air the still plain had and the silent roads. All lay as if enchained, motionless, sound-less, as if weighed down by an invisible and crushing force.

But presently over the distance of the plain came the sound of a midnight bell ; and from the other end, as though to meet it, floated another, and after it a third, a fourth. On the dark background of the night stood out clear-burning the glowing spires of churches, and the country awoke suddenly to life. Along the roads began to stretch long lines of villages. First walked the poor, those worn by work and want, with bleeding hearts and drooping heads. These were bringing to the temple their humility and their sorrow ; this was all they had to give to the God Who had arisen. Next, after them, and at some distance, followed in their holiday garb the rich, the oppressors, and all the powerful of the village. They chattered gaily to each other. They were bringing to the temple their thoughts of the week's merry-making.[1] But soon the crowds of peasantry were swallowed in the distance of the road, the last sound of the church bell died away into the air, and all once more returned to a solemnity of silence.

And as all movement stopped, there came the sense of profound mystery, as if after the silence that had fallen, a miracle was about to happen—a miracle which would breathe life into all things.

And it was so.

Scarcely had the East time to redden than the wished-for miracle happened.

The Crucified and the Insulted God arose. The God to Whom the wretched and the sick at heart from the first beginnings of times have cried, ' Lord, haste Thee ! '

God arose, and straightway filled the Universe with Himself. The broad steppe rose to meet Him with all its snows and storms. Beyond the steppe stretched far the mighty forest, seeming to feel the presence of Him Who had risen. The ancient firs lifted to heaven their hoary arms ; the hundred-year-old pines creaking swayed their heads ; the ravines and rivers sent forth a roar, and beasts ran out from holes and lairs, and birds

---

[1] Easter Sunday in Russia brings, after the Great Fast, a week of feasting and gaiety. It is the great holiday of the year.—*Tr.*

from nests ; all felt that from the depth was coming something of light and strength, something that gave out light and warmth, and all cried, ' Lord, is it Thou ? '

God blessed the earth and the waters, and the beasts, the warmth and the sun, and said to them :

' Peace be with you ! I have brought you Spring and warmth and light. I will lift from the rivers their chains of ice, and clothe the steppe with a green coverlet, and fill the forest with singing and with lovely scents. I will give meat and drink to the birds and to the beasts, and fill all Nature with joyousness. Her laws shall be light for you. About every blade of grass and every smallest insect she shall draw bounds within which they shall remain true to their ordained purpose. You cannot be judged, for you but fulfil the destiny that has been given you since the beginning of time. Man carries on a ceaseless struggle with Nature, fathoming her secrets and seeing no end to his labours. The knowledge of these secrets is necessary to him ; to his well-being and success. But Nature is self-sufficient and therein lies her strength. It matters little to her that man probes into her depths. He subdues only atoms, and Nature still stands unapproachable as before, and crushes him with her might. Peace be with you, steppes and forests, beasts and feathered ones ! Be warmed in the rays of My Resurrection ! '

Having blessed Nature, the Lord turned to men. First came out to Him the suffering, those bent under the burden of toil and destroyed by want. And when He said to them, ' Peace be with you ! ' they filled the air with sobbing and fell down before Him, mutely asking for deliverance.

And the Lord's heart was once more clouded by that great, that mortal anguish with which it had filled to overflowing in the Garden of Gethsemane in expectation of the cup ordained for Him. This host of the much-suffering which now fell low before Him bore the burden of life truly for His sake ; they were always the first to listen to His word, and it was for ever imprinted on their hearts. He had seen them all from the heights of Golgotha, had seen how distractedly they ran to and fro, enmeshed in the nets of slavery, and He had blessed them all on His way to the Cross ; He promised freedom to them all. And since that day they all thirst for Him, all strive towards Him. With boundless faith they all stretch out their arms to Him—' Lord, is it Thou ? '

' Yes, it is I,' He said to them. ' I have broken the chains of Death in order to come to you, My faithful servants, dear fellow-sufferers ! I am always and every-where with you, and where your blood is shed, there Mine is shed with yours. You with clean heart have limitless faith in Me, only because My preaching con-tains the Truth, without which the universe holds nothing but destruction and chaos. Love God, and love thy neighbour as thyself—this is the truth in all its clearness and simplicity, and it is clearest not to priests and teachers but verily unto you, simple and sorrowing hearts. In summer, under the scorching sun, behind the plough, you serve it ; in the long evenings of winter, by the light of the smoking wood-torch, at your meagre supper you teach it to your children. Brief though it is, for you it holds the whole meaning of life and the endless source of fresh and fresher discussions. With this Truth you arise in the morning, with it you lie down at night to sleep, and it you bring as offering to the altar in the form of tears and sighs, which, sweeter than the odour of incense, opens My heart. Know then—although no man knows beforehand when your hour will come, it is near. This longed-for hour will strike, and light shall come, which no darkness can conquer. And you shall cast from you the burden of grief, and need, and misery, the burden that crushes you now. I affirm this. Heretofore I blessed you to gain your souls, I bless you now for a new life in the kingdom of light and goodness and truth. May your hearts be not turned aside by words of guile, may they be always clean and simple as ever they have been, and My word shall be Truth. Peace be with you ! '

The Lord proceeded and met others on His way. These were the rich, and the oppressors, the cruel rulers, the hypocrites, the false, the bigoted, and the unjust. They all walked with hearts of dust, and chatted merrily together, welcoming not the Resurrection, but the coming worldly holiday. But they too stopped in consternation as they felt the approach of Him Who had risen.

He stopped before them also, and said :

' Ye are men of this age, and by the spirit of the age are ye guided. Strife and self-interest—these are the springs of your actions. Evil has filled the whole sum of your lives, but you can bear the yoke of evil so lightly that not a scruple has made your conscience tremble at what that yoke prepares for you. All things about you seem to be called to serve you. But you possess the world not by your own strength, but by the power you have inherited from your forefathers. Since then you have been protected on all sides, and the mighty of the earth deem you eternal. Since then with fire and sword you have gone on and on, robbing and killing, belching forth blasphemy against the laws of God and man, boasting that such was your immemorial, inherited right. But I say unto you, the time shall come, and it is not far distant, when your vain hopes shall be scattered as dust, and the weak shall know their strength, and you shall acknowledge that weakness before your strength. Have you ever foreseen that dread hour ? Has ever that prevision troubled you for yourselves and for your children ? '

The sinful were silent. They stood with downcast heads, as if waiting something bitterer still.

Then He Who had arisen continued :

' But in the name of the Resurrection I open even to you a way of salvation—this is the judgment of your own conscience. It will show to you your past in all its nakedness ; it will call up before you the shades of those you have destroyed, and will put them as sentinels at your bed-head. The gnashing of teeth shall fill your homes. Wives shall not know their husbands, nor children their fathers. But when your heart shall be withered with anguish and sorrow, when your conscience shall be full to overflowing, like a cup which can hold no more of the bitterness that fills it—then the shades of those you have destroyed shall make their peace with you and open the way to your salvation. And then there shall be no more hypocrites, nor oppressors, nor extortioners, nor bigots, nor unjust rulers, and all alike shall joyfully sit down at meat together with Me. Go then, and know that My word is—Truth!'

At that moment the East reddened and from the thinning darkness of the forest stood out a hideous human mass, swinging upon an aspen. The head of the hanged man, all but severed from the body, hung downward; the ravens had already pecked out the eyes and eaten away the cheeks. The trunk itself, in places bare of clothing and gaping with festering wounds, waved its arms in the wind. Birds of prey circled above it, and the bolder of these continued their work of destruction.

This was the body of the betrayer who had done judgment on himself.

All present turned away with horror and disgust from the sight before them. The eyes of Him Who had arisen were fired with wrath.

'Betrayer!' He said, 'you thought by self-inflicted death to rid yourself of the burden of treason which weighed you down; you soon were aware of your disgrace and made haste to close accounts with a shameful life. Your crime so clearly rose before you that you fell back in horror before the world's contempt, and chose instead your soul's destruction. " One moment," you said to yourself, " and my soul shall plunge into

244

irrevocable eternal darkness, and my heart cease to feel the pangs of conscience." But that shall not be so. Come down from the tree, betrayer, and may sight return to your hollow eyes, and may your festering wounds now close, and may your shameful body take on the form it had at the moment you kissed Him you betrayed. Live ! '

At this word, before the eyes of all, the betrayer came down from the tree, and fell upon the ground before the Lord, imploring Him to give him back death.

' I have shown to all the way of salvation,' continued the Lord, ' but for you, betrayer, it is closed for ever. You are accursed of God and man, accursed for everlasting. You did not kill your friend when he had opened his heart to you, but took him unawares and gave him up to be done to death and to be insulted. For this I condemn you to life. You shall go from town to town for ever and ever, and nowhere shall you find a roof to shelter you. You shall knock at doors, and no one shall open ; you shall beg for bread, and be given a stone ; you shall thirst, and shall be given a vessel filled with the blood of Him you have betrayed. You shall weep, and your tears shall turn into fiery streams, scorching and scarring your cheeks. The stones upon which you walk shall cry out, " Betrayer, be accursed ! " The crowd in the market-place shall part before you, and on all faces you shall read, " Betrayer, be accursed ! " You shall seek death on land and water, and everywhere death shall turn from you, hissing, " Betrayer, be accursed ! " Moreover, for a little space, fate shall take pity on you, you shall get a friend, and shall betray him, and from the depth of his dungeon this friend shall cry, " Betrayer, be accursed ! " You shall have power to do good, but it shall turn away the hearts of those you have done good to. " Be accursed ! " they shall all cry, " be accursed, you and all your works ! " And you shall go for everlasting with a never-ceasing worm gnawing your heart, with a ruined soul. Live, betrayer, and be for future generations a witness of that endless punishment which awaits treachery. Arise, take for a staff the branch on which you thought to find death—and go ! '

And scarcely had the words of the Lord died away on the air than the betrayer arose from the ground, took up his staff, and soon the sound of his footsteps merged into the silence of that infinite, mysterious distance where awaited for him everlasting life. And he walks the earth even to this day, sowing confusion, treachery, and strife. . . .

THE VIRTUES AND THE VICES

THE Virtues had from times immemorial been at
enmity with the Vices. The Vices led a merry life and
managed their affairs neatly, while the Virtues led a
greyer existence, but on the other hand, in all the
reading-books and anthologies they were held up as
models for imitation. But on the quiet they used nevertheless to think, ' It would be nice like the Vices to
pull off a little affair or two.' And to tell the truth,
while the noise was going on they did pull some off.

It is difficult to say what began their quarrel first, and
who started it. I think it was the Virtues who began
it. Vice is a nippy beggar, and quick to think of things.
When he set off like a racehorse, spanking along to show
off in the wide world, dressed in gold and silk, the
Virtues could not keep up with him. And not being
able to keep up, they got huffy. ' All right ! ' they
said, ' show off in your silk and gold, brazen-face ! We
even in rags shall be respected by all.' And the Vices
said to them, ' Oh, go and be respected, do ! '

The Virtues could not bear the taunt and began to
scold the Vices at every cross-road. They would come
out in tatters at the crossing and accost the passers-by
continually, ' Isn't it true, good people, honest folk,
that you love us even in tatters ? ' And the passers-by
would answer, ' What a heap of you beggarwomen there
are nowadays ! Move on, don't delay us. God will
give to you.'

They tried, the Virtues, to get help from the police too. ' What are you about ? You have let the public go anyhow ! Why, it will be up to its ears in Vice if you don't look out.' But the policemen just stood there, touching their hats to the Vices.

And so the Virtues got nothing out of it and only said with chagrin, ' You wait ! You 'll get sentenced to hard labour for your doings ! '

But the Vices, in the meantime, just went ahead— boasting about it too ! ' There 's a thing to threaten us with—hard labour ! We may get hard labour, or we may not, but you have been up to your ears in it from your birth. Oh, you spiteful things—look at them : skin and bone, and their eyes burning like coals. They champ their teeth at a tart but don't know how to set to work eating it.'

In fact, the strife grew from day to day. Time and again it came to blows, and even here Fortune betrayed the Virtues. The Vices would get the best of it, and put the Virtues in irons. ' There, sit quiet, you mischief-makers ! ' And there they would sit till the Authorities interfered, and let them go.

During one of these battles Ivan-the-fool happened to come by, and says he to the combatants :

' Stupids, you are stupids ! What on earth are you injuring each other for ? In the beginning of things you were all just *qualities*—only afterwards, from human foolishness and quibbling, it turned into Virtues and Vices. Some got too much restriction put on them, others got too much way on, and so the wheels of the machine went wrong. And there was born into the world disturbance, strife, and sorrow. . . . I 'll tell you what to do : get back to the primary source, and maybe you 'll find something to agree upon.'

He said this and went his way to take his tax to the Treasury.

Whether Ivan's words had effect on the combatants, or they had not breath to go on fighting, anyway they sheathed their swords and fell a-thinking.

To be sure it was mostly the Virtues who did the thinking, because their stomachs were very empty ; but the Vices, as soon as the bugles sounded the retreat, went off to their wicked occupations and began to live merrily as before.

'It 's all very fine, this talking of qualities,' Humility began. 'We know all about these " qualities "—only one lot of qualities go swaggering about in velvet and eat off gold dishes and the others have to dress in sacking and go without a meal for days together. It 's nothing to Ivànoushka when he has stuffed himself with bran, and he is right to be sure—but you can't keep *us* on bran—we know what 's what ! '

'And what are these same " qualities " that have appeared ? ' Seemliness joined in, alarmed. 'Is there a catch in it somewhere ? There have always been Virtues and Vices—hundreds of thousands of years this has been going on, and hundreds of thousands of books have been written about it, and he has solved it in an instant—" qualities ! " You just dip into these

hundreds of thousands of books and you 'll see what a
dust there 'll be raised from them ! '

They thought and discussed and at last came to this
conclusion : Seemliness was right. How many thousand
centuries Virtues have been classed as Virtues and Vices
as Vices. Virtues have always stood on the right and
Vices on the left, and suddenly by Ivànoushka's fool
word—give everything up and call yourself some kind
of ' quality ' ! Why, that would be almost like giving
up your estate and calling yourself a human ! Simple,
of course, but some simplicity is worse than thieving, as
the saying goes. No, it was no use to think of
' qualities '—but a compromise of some sort now—
that would give the Virtues a better time and suit the
Vices too—that 'll be business. Because the Vices,
after all, do have a poor time of it sometimes !

The other day, for instance, Lechery was caught in the
act in the bath-house, and was run in, and Adultery kicked
downstairs in his shirt, and Freethinking, that had but
lately bloomed luxuriantly, was now plucked up by the
roots. So that it could not but be an advantage to the
Vices, too, to effect a compromise. Ladies and gentlemen, would any one like to propose a little ' method ' ?

In response to this appeal, there stepped forward a very
old man—Experience, he was called. (There are two
Experiences—one virtuous and the other vicious. This
was the virtuous one.) And he proposed this little plan :

' Find,' he said, ' a treasure which both the Virtues
respect and the Vices would not be averse to. And
send him as an envoy to the enemy's camp.'

They set to work searching, and of course found it. They found two hacks—Moderation and Precision. They both lived in back paddocks behind the Virtues' village, held the orphan's share of land, but traded in smuggled vodka and received the Vices on the quiet.

However, the first attempt was a failure. The hacks were not much to look at, and were too yielding to carry out what they had been entrusted with. Hardly had they appeared in the Vices' camp, hardly had they begun to palaver : ' A little is more comfortable and the quieter the surer,' when the whole crowd of Vices began yelling, ' We know these proverbs. You 've been hanging round with them this long time, but we weren't born yesterday. Go home, old jades, and don't eat your bread without earning it.'

And, as if to show the Virtues that they were not to be taken in, they rolled into the pub ' Samarkand ' for the whole night, and going their ways in the morning, caught Temperance and Continence and treated them so shamefully that even the Tartars in the ' Samarkand ' were astonished—' pleasant gentlemen, but how they do go on ! '

Then the Virtues understood that it was a grave matter, and that they must set to work seriously.

There appeared among them at this time a neuter sort of being, not a crab, nor a fish, nor a hen, nor a bird, nor a lady, nor a gentleman, but a little of all of these. It appeared, grew, and matured. And its name was Hypocrisy.

Everything about this being was a mystery—includ-

251

ing its origin. The old folks did say that once Meekness
and Lechery came together in a dark passage and this
was the fruit of their union. This the Virtues brought
up between them and then sent to boarding-school, to
the Frenchwoman Madame Comme-il-faut. The con-
jecture was confirmed also by Hypocrisy's appearance,
because, although it always went about with downcast
eyes, the sharp ones noticed that sensual shadows often
flitted across its face, and its back now and again had
quite an unpleasant wriggle. Doubtless Hypocrisy owed
its dual appearance largely to the influence of the
boarding-school Comme-il-faut. There it learnt all the
chief sciences—how to look as if ' butter wouldn't melt
in its mouth,' how to ' worm its way in,' and how to
' lick boots ' as well—in fact, everything which can ensure virtuous living. But at the same time it did not
escape the ' cancan ' influence, with which the walls and
the air of the boarding-school were saturated. Moreover, Madame Comme-il-faut made matters worse by
telling Hypocrisy facts about its parents—she had to
acknowledge that the father (Lechery) was very ' mau-
vais ton,' and impertinent—would keep pinching everybody ; about the mother (Meekness) that although she
had not a striking appearance, she screamed so prettily
when pinched that even those Vices not naturally pre-
disposed to pinching, such as Venality, Arrogance,
Despondency, etc.—even they were not able to forgo
that pleasure.

So this neuter being, with downcast eyes but glances
wandering from under drooping lashes to see how the

land lay, the Virtues chose to parley with the Vices, and to invent a *modus vivendi* which would enable both to live at ease.

'But can you behave like us?' Good Manners thought to ask, as a preliminary examination.

'I?' asked Hypocrisy, astonished. 'I'll do this.'

And before the Virtues could turn round, Hypocrisy's eyes were cast down, its hands crossed on its breast, and on its cheeks a gentle flush . . . a maid indeed!

'Goodness, the jade! Well now—and like them?'

But Hypocrisy did not even reply. In one moment it had done something not actually visible to the eye, but so convincing that Sharpsightedness only spat.

If you've put your hand to the plough there's no turning back: humiliating as it was, they had to beg the Vices' forgiveness. Hypocrisy, going to their nefarious den, did not know where to look. 'Everywhere this beastliness,' it said aloud, and to itself, 'Ah, the Vices do live well!' And indeed, hardly had Hypocrisy gone a mile from the Virtues' residence, than all round it flooded a sea of laughter, song, dance, and gaming— a very din of merriment. And an excellent town the Vices had built for themselves too: spacious, light, with big streets and little, with squares and boulevards. There was the Street of Falsewitness, Treachery Square, and Shameful Boulevard. The 'Father of Lies' himself sat here, and from a little shop sold Calumny on draught and in bottle.

But though the Vices lived merrily and though they were so experienced in all kinds of iniquity, when they

saw Hypocrisy they raised their hands. To look at, it
was truly a maiden—and yet was it ?—the devil himself
could not have told. Even the Father of Lies, who
thought there was no beastliness on earth he could not
get to the bottom of, even *his* eyes started out of his head.

' Well,' he said, ' it was a vain dream of mine that
there was no one on earth more harmful than I. I ?—
Why, *this* is the real poison of poisons. I am only a
brazen-face, and that 's how now and again—though not
often—I get kicked downstairs—but this treasure—if it
lays a-hold of you there 's no getting rid of it ! It 'll so
get round you and about you and tangle you up, that
till it sucks the life-blood out of you it won't let you go ! '

Nevertheless, although great was the enthusiasm
roused by Hypocrisy, even here there were differences
of opinion. The more solid Vices (the aborigines), who
valued above everything the traditions of the past, as
Sophistry, Vainglory, Pride, Misanthropy, and so on, not
only did not go to meet Hypocrisy, but even warned
others against it.

' True Vices have no need of being hidden,' they said,
' but hold their banner high and terrifyingly. What of
importance can Hypocrisy show us that we have not
known and practised from the beginning of time ?
Absolutely nothing. On the contrary, it teaches us
dangerous subterfuges and will end by making us, if
not ashamed of ourselves, at any rate seem to be
ashamed. *Caveant consules !* Hitherto we have had
many trusty followers, but they, seeing our subterfuges,
may say, " The Vices must have been having a pretty

poor time, since they have got to disown themselves!"
And they will turn from them, turn from them.'

So spoke the inveterate Vices, who acknowledged no
new tendencies, allurements, or circumstances. Having
been born in dirt, they preferred to be smothered in it
rather than abandon ancient tradition.

After them came another category of Vices, who also
did not show much enthusiasm on meeting Hypocrisy,
but not, however, because they disliked it, but because
they already had without its aid secret relations with
the Virtues. Such were Falseness, Perfidy, Treachery,
Slander, Calumny, etc. They did not break out into
exclamations of triumph, or into applause or congratula-
tions, but simply winked ' Walk in ! '

However, Hypocrisy's triumph was assured. The
young ones, like Adultery, Drunkenness, Brawling, etc.,
at once called a meeting and greeted the envoy with
such ovations that Sophistry was obliged to stop its
grumbling for ever.

' You only muddle every one, old wretches ! ' the
young ones shouted to the old people. ' We want to
live, and you just depress us all ! We shall get into the
reading-books (this was especially flattering), we shall
shine in drawing-rooms ! Old ladies will love us.'

In short, ground for agreement was found at once, so
that when Hypocrisy, having returned, gave the Virtues
an account of its mission, it was unanimously acknowledged that all grounds for the existence of Virtues and
Vices as separate and inimical groups was removed for
ever. Nevertheless, they did not venture to do away

with the old nomenclature—it might be needed again, who knows ?—but determined to use it so sparingly that it should be evident to every one that it covered only dust and ashes.

From this time there was much entertainment between the Virtues and the Vices. If Dissoluteness wanted to go and see Continence, he just took Hypocrisy on his arm, and Continence seeing them from afar would welcome them.

' Oh, do come in ! Pray walk in. We have heard of you. . . .'

And the other way round too. If Abstinence wanted to taste a forbidden sweet at Dissoluteness's, she would take Hypocrisy on her arm, and Dissoluteness would fling open the door.

' Oh, do come in ! Pray walk in. We have heard of you. . . .'

On fast days they fed with discretion, on frugal days modestly . . . with one hand they made the sign of the Cross, with the other committed furious deeds. One eye they raised to Heaven, and with the other they lusted. For the first time the Virtues knew Frailty, and the Vices were not out of pocket. On the contrary, they told every one they met they were having the time of their lives.

And Ivànoushka the fool cannot to this day understand why the Virtues and the Vices made friends through Hypocrisy when it was so much more natural through their all being just ' qualities.'

A translation of Shchedrin's novel
THE GOLOVLYOV FAMILY
by Natalie A. Duddington is published
by Messrs. George Allen & Unwin
Ltd.

Printed in Great Britain
by T. and A. CONSTABLE LTD.
at the University Press
Edinburgh